The Bodle

C000137941

other **Oxford** stories

The Bodleian Murders
&
other **Oxford** stories

OxPens

First published in Great Britain 2010 by OxPens in conjunction with WritersPrintShop

ISBN 9781904623243

Designed by Ant Creative London
The cover image is by Valerie Petts and is reproduced by very kind permission of the artist.
These stories are works of fiction and the characters and events in them exist only in their pages and in the authors' imagination.
The profits from this book will be shared with Oxford Homeless Pathways (formerly Oxford Night Shelter).

Contents

SYMPATHETIC MAGIC

ALISON HOBLYN

Once there was a woman - well, actually there still is - but this history begins a few years ago. This woman was young (if twenty-eight is young to you) and lovely; and by that I mean, not only did she have classic beauty, but she did not have a mean-spirited bone in her body either. She lived in the city of Alice and Dreaming Spires (as opposed to the city of badly-repaired roads and social deprivation) because she was a member of the teaching faculty of the ancient University of Oxford. Yes, clever too! But not proud. This delight of a woman saw herself to be at the service of her students and they, in return, loved her.

As befits such a porcelain creature, there was a man who fell in love with her when she was in her prime. She was studying for her doctorate and he for his when he annexed her for his very own. If the truth be told, she waited more than three years for him to ask the question she hoped for. He, being the type to think deeply and widely, wading the slow river of his academic mind, cogitated long and hard before he did indeed finally propose: it was not so much "pop" the question as dredge it from the silt. This rite at last completed, our heroine waited to settle into a time of deep contentment: but, alas, the state did not seem to arrive. It was like a tide that never came in, the waters glistening tantalisingly on the horizon.

She worked hard in the groves of academe; toiling tirelessly. Here too disappointment lurked in the fertile orchards. Somehow her reward seemed to be confined to picking up windfalls while her male colleagues in the cloistered gardens plucked golden apples from ever-higher boughs. She did not begrudge her beloved his successes, for she felt she partook of them in their union. She gladly attended functions in his college to support his advance (although, it has to be said, he was less enthusiastic about reciprocal events, declaring that he 'had issues' with some

1

of the dons at her place of work). Sometimes she would stand alone and gaze through the ancient glass in the stone-mullioned windows, watching the outside world distorted through the lens of a rippled pane, and wonder where her brains had led her. She enjoyed the young students and gave them her time, while they gave her a glimpse of heartfelt spontaneity that seemed to have passed her by.

Another year passed, each of them caught up in the demands of their work. He did suggest they moved in to a place together, and she was more than happy to be the one to add all the touches that made the rented house a home. Three-bedroomed in the Iffley Road: she dared even to think of a life with children. Against the day when there would be one salary, she also took on some private tutoring in the vacations, seeing Oxbridge candidates in the bijou semi's front room. He was getting busier and the date for the wedding remained on hold while invitations to conferences and submissions of papers were accepted, attended and completed. She was filled with pride, watching him making presentations, casual but smart in his suit and t-shirt, navy blue against the tan of his skin. It was easy to be proud of him, if not for herself. Her own work reviews came and went: many smiles, a kind word here and there, but a mere nod to her research.

One day when she was tutoring in her college room, a knock came at her door.

'I'm the carpenter,' he said.

She'd forgotten the bursar had made this appointment.

'Do you have to do this now? I'm just finishing a tutorial.'

'Don't mind me,' he said with a disarming smile. 'It's only some measuring. Very quiet.'

So she stepped back to let him in and resumed her place with the student. Ten minutes later the boy gathered up his leaves of paper, packing them into his bag with thanks and a shy smile to his tutor. He left the panelled room and clattered down the stone stairway to the real world.

'Very good.' He was speaking to her. She looked up from her desk at the carpenter.

'What?' she said.

'The way you spoke to that boy.'

The lovely woman was speechless apart from a small 'Oh.'

In another ten minutes he was gone, leaving nothing but traces of warmth.

It was autumn now and a chill was encroaching on the days. Another gathering of fine minds in another European city had taken her fiancé away and she sat with one more Oxbridge hopeful in her front room (the study would not accommodate two) and watched the rain trickle down the window. And so the days passed through to winter, when beloved was adopted as a media darling. The man was full of ideas and concepts; his intellect vomited them up unstoppably, leaving room for more. Now she sat and watched his face on BBC Four with a mix of pride and longing. Her 31st birthday had come and gone, as had several more potential dates for a wedding. The latter seemed insignificant now that they had settled into the domestic round, comfortable and convivial. But the third bedroom in the Iffley Road began to exert its spell upon her. When he returned from Vienna, she would put it to him.

He told her, in the bleak hinterland of post-Christmas, that he was leaving her. He couldn't express why, exactly, but he had thought about it long and hard and knew that this was the right decision. Despite the sensation of her legs giving way beneath her and a brick where her heart should be, she summoned enough presence to "thank" him for all the intellect he had applied to this decision but wondered aloud why - for a man who attended so many conferences - he had not thought to confer with her. She, after all, had a mind equal to, and maybe surpassing, his.

For once there was silence. Answering questions directly is not the province of the academic. (Later, a very good woman friend of his opined that he had been tortured by the whole event and that she was helping him to come to terms with it.)

In February, living with chill in her house and in her heart, the lovely creature went out as often as possible for consolation. When her many friends were unavailable she wandered the museums. In the Pitt-Rivers one day she was engaged by a case labelled "Sympathetic Magic". There was a wooden fish, beautifully carved by Native American Indians, said by them to attract spawning salmon to the point in the river where it was placed. There were small silver votive pieces in the shape of an eye, a liver, a heart, which were offered up for prayer by South American Catholics. New life and healing would come to that part of the body thus offered, they believed. The way these hopes, wishes and dreams were made into something solid attached itself to her heart with but a fleeting excursion to her intellect.

In April, as she sat in her college rooms, through yet another week of hammering and sawing inflicted by the maintenance team, now in their second month of occupation, she was able to smile through the inconvenience. She punctuated her study hours (a bright new project had prolonged these to her satisfaction) with excursions to the Botanic Garden across the way. There she could actually see the spring returning in small seedlings and dwarf tulips. Within the boundaries of the stone walls, thrushes and blackbirds echoed her blossoming joy. Dormant plants were beginning to send up attention-seeking shoots. New life was what she craved and she conjured up the third bedroom in her mind. It was in the Botanic Garden that she learned of the Doctrine of Signatures. As a 'physic' garden in the 1700s, many of its plants had been used for medicinal purposes. It was deemed that if a plant resembled a body part it had some affinity with it: indeed this was a 'sign' that it had been created to do good for the health of mankind. She studied the spotted leaves of the lungwort - so called because its leaves were meant to resemble diseased lungs - and later researched the male-like shape of the mandrake root, finding that infertile women in medieval times slept with it under their pillows at night. In each case she mused upon the metaphysical coalescence of name and effect.

By May the spring sun was developing heat and the garden in the Iffley Road was transforming. She had, with the thoroughness of an academically-trained mind, found exactly the plants she wanted. Myosotis 'Baby Blue' - the sky-coloured forget-me-not - was frothing around her tulips. Phormium tenax 'Bronze Baby' shot out from pots on the terrace that was edged with Bergenia 'Baby Doll', now flowering in shades of soft pink. New shoots surged from the ground where Baby's Breath would soon be a white sheet of blossom. The daylight hours grew longer and the summer was a time of contentment; hot slow days accompanied by distant sounds; bees droning, a saw plying through timber. She picked posies of Baby Sunrose, Gaillardia 'Baby Cole', Hebe 'Baby Blush' and Rose 'Baby Masquerade', dead-heading assiduously and mulching her plants with sawdust. Perfume infused the still of the night and the green throated Hemerocallis 'Lullaby Baby' glowed in the light of a harvest moon. In the third bedroom she tended the tumbling greenery of the Baby's Tears pot plant and placed delicately carved wooden babies on the windowsill. On hot days when the breeze flickered, she sat at the open study window and concentrated steadily on her paper. Her creative roots worked deep and, looking into the garden, she felt everything growing without and within.

In the late days of October her paper was published and then presented to her peers. She knew how good it was by the strong feelings it elicited; no more patronising smiles, and the silence from the ex-beloved was more than satisfying. But this, she knew, was not to be her best production. By late November the leaves had fled the trees revealing a clean parchment of skyline. As she began to appreciate the way the frosted branches scribbled new lines in December, she left the Iffley Road for a day or so and went up the hill to Headington. On her return she had an occupant for the third bedroom and a beautifully made crib to lay her in.

Maybe it was a little sympathetic magic that brought this new life - it's up to you what you believe and how you read the story. What can be told is this: as the moon shone in the window of the three-bedroomed house in the Iffley Road, anyone in the dark street below would have beheld the lady, the carpenter and their baby, ready to live happily ever after.

A VISIT FROM SOCIAL SERVICES

SHEILA COSTELLO

In the last remaining seconds before the social worker appeared, Eric Pledge contrived to hide the dead mouse. He dropped it into the nearest receptacle, his mother's favourite teapot, and as he replaced the lid the knock came.

Eric hastened to the door. It was raining. It had not stopped raining for a week. Before the door could be opened there was the metal barrier that he'd installed as part of the flood defences to be levered out of the way, and half a dozen sandbags to be kicked aside. Through the spyhole he saw the young, slightly crumpled face of Tim Dawson from Social Services. Tim had made it across the moat then. Eric was gratified. He'd dug the moat this week and laid a plank across to serve as a bridge. It was killing work. The arthritis in his fingers had plagued him horribly.

Tim stepped over the threshold, puppyish and eager to please. 'Very nice moat, Eric. You've done wonders improving the defences.'

Eric nodded. 'Case of having to. The Thames is rising. All the rain.'

'South Oxford,' said Tim. 'Watery place.'

'Not only the Thames,' said Eric. 'There's the Trill Mill stream running wild, and various tributaries.'

'Nightmare,' said Tim. 'Don't know how you cope. Be like a fortress round here soon.'

Eric took this as a compliment. Tim wasn't a bad sort. They'd rubbed along together pretty well since old Mrs Pledge began to fail and he'd had to call in help. Tim was friendly and obliging, though sometimes he did seem a little innocent about the ways of the world.

Today's visit was crucial. The assessment of Mrs Pledge's eligibility for admission to a care home. Eric always made sure the house was neat and tidy when Social Services called. The discovery of a deceased member of the vermin class fifteen minutes ago had interfered with his routine. He didn't want anything around that might lower the tone. As Tim hovered by the entrance, Eric found himself checking for signs of mouse droppings or unwelcome rodent bodies in the hall.

Tim cleared his throat and asked how Mrs Pledge was doing.

'Mother's in the sitting room,' said Eric, battling a strong urge to fall on all fours and inspect the area behind the shoe rack.

'Should I go through?'

'Yes,' said Eric with a furtive twitch at the curtain draped across the sandbags by the door.

In the sitting room Mrs Pledge was spread out in a wheelchair, apparently asleep.

'Mother has drifted into a decline,' Eric said, settling himself at the table beside his visitor. 'Daily she is weakening. Look at her poor thin arms. She's not much more than a heap of bones.'

Tim Dawson clucked sympathetically. 'You've done her proud so far, Eric, but it really can't go on like this. She needs a higher level of care. Fortunately, there are several homes in the city offering full nursing support - '

Eric felt a spasm of trepidation. It suddenly struck him what might be coming next. That place up the road. Convenient in some ways but there were rumours locally.

'The obvious choice in your case,' Tim went on, unaware of his client's inner turmoil, 'could well be Humpty Dumpty House.'

The air froze, the room span giddily.

Eric swallowed and whispered, 'I don't want to be awkward, Tim, but I'm not sure I'd be quite comfortable putting Mother into Humpty Dumpty House. Round here they say - '

'They say what?'

'They say,' whispered Eric, 'that the residents suffer a disproportionate number of falls.'

The social worker blanched and his lips began to tremble. 'This is dreadful, dreadful. I'll speak to my boss. There'll have to be an investigation.'

'Besides,' whispered Eric, ' how could I keep respect in the community if Mother went into a place called Humpty Dumpty House? It's such a stupid name.'

Tim rolled his eyes. 'It's these new Naming Committees. They're coming in all over the country now. Naming is being contracted out. The councils claim it's cheaper that way. Of course, here in Oxford, the committee is very hot on culture.'

'I thought it was bad enough,' said Eric, 'when our address changed to Hatter Drive. We used to be Hawthorn Avenue.'

'The Naming Executive for the South ward is an Alice fan,' said Tim. 'Count yourself lucky, Eric. My auntie's moved to the Lake District. There's a Beatrix Potter enthusiast up there. My auntie lives in Tiggywinkle Walk.'

Eric privately wondered how the new committees would cope in areas where they didn't give a toss about culture but said nothing. Tim pressed on. Flushed with embarrassment, he haltingly informed his client that the Upper East ward boasted a Tolkien expert and found the courage to ask whether Mrs Pledge might be happy to end her days in the Bilbo Baggins Care Facility in Headington. From the depths of the wheelchair came a gurgle and something that sounded vaguely like a laugh.

'Save us!' cried Eric in alarm. 'Was that the death rattle I heard? Has Mother passed?'

Mrs Pledge reverted to snoring.

'I feared that the mention of hobbits had led to a crisis,' Eric went on, wiping his brow. 'Mother has a phobia about short, stumpy people. I had to dispose of my collection of painted gnomes last summer. They were getting to her. Under the circumstances, I don't think the Bilbo Baggins Facility would be at all suitable, Tim.'

He downed a glass of soda water. The general agitation was making him restless again. What were those dark little pellets on the rug? He hadn't noticed them before. He leapt up. 'I'll just fetch the vacuum. The carpet needs doing. Won't be long.'

As the door closed, Mrs Pledge opened her eyes and said, 'Eric is such a fusser. He fusses about everything. He's obsessive. It's a shame.'

The social worker, propelled into a conversation that he hadn't expected, answered, 'You're awake now, are you, Mrs Pledge? That's good.'

'I've been awake all along,' the old lady said. 'Sometimes it's best to be a listener. I threw in a few snoring noises for the sake of form.'

The social worker remembered his training and the stress laid on being affirmative. 'You snore very well, Mrs Pledge,' he said.

Mrs Pledge thanked him and said she was at a bit of a loose end at the moment. 'Stuck in this chair with Eric fussing round. Oh, Eric's decent. He looks after me properly. I shouldn't complain. But he doesn't understand that I have requirements.' She lowered her voice. 'The problem is, when you get to my age sex isn't so easy to come by any more. I was hoping that if we could find the right care home - '

Tim Dawson plunged into his briefcase and rummaged for the training manual. He always carried it round. A paragraph heading on page twenty-four, *Physical Activity and the Elderly*, ordered him to be sensitive when dealing with delicate issues. He coughed and spluttered and finally wrote in his notes: *Mrs Pledge seems lonely and in need of stimulation*. Eric, trudging in with the vacuum, gave the notes a quick glance.

'I would change that sentence if I were you,' he said.

Mrs Pledge, to all appearances, had now gone back to sleep. Eric directed the vacuum nozzle at the suspect patch of rug. Tim the social worker fretted over his syntax. Through the window Eric saw that the rain had turned to hail and that the water was almost level with the top of the moat.

'I'll have to open the sluice gates and let the flood into the drainage channel,' he gasped.

'The sluice gates?' muttered Tim Dawson, looking up.

'I installed them on Wednesday,' said Eric, dashing out.

Once he'd gone Mrs Pledge's eyelids flickered and she winked. 'Bless him,' she said. 'He means well, he wouldn't harm a fly. Now to return to our previous discussion. I'm perfectly willing to go into a home. Indeed, I would be overjoyed to go into a home. But it has to be the ideal home. I'm looking for company and a little flirtation. I'm afraid the Bilbo Baggins won't do. I can't stand small, stocky men. They always suffer personal hygiene problems. As for the Humpty Dumpty, I have to say I wouldn't be seen dead in that place. You must have somewhere else you can suggest.'

Tim leafed through his folder. 'There is Narnia -'

'Where?'

'Narnia. Up in Risinghurst. Very select. You get a lot of North Oxford people booking in there. The male residents tend to be dons and professors, superior types. They've taken care of themselves over the years so they - ' How to put it? It was difficult. 'They are still capable of relishing vigorous pursuits.'

Mrs Pledge looked delighted at the prospect.

'The Naming Executive for the Outer East ward is keen on C.S. Lewis and he takes a great interest in the home. Narnia has all the latest features. Fitted kitchens, a sauna and spa, a sun lounge. Each bedroom is individually-designed with a king-size bed and built-in wardrobes - '

'That's the one. It's got everything I want,' said Mrs Pledge, rubbing her hands. 'I can't wait. Narnia sounds like an old woman's dream. You did say the male residents were youthful in aspect, didn't you? Splendid. Why don't we have a cup of tea to celebrate?'

'Allow me,' said Tim.

'Not at all. I can manage the business of making tea. Eric will have it that I'm frail and weak but the fact is that I'm sinewy. I play the part while he's around to keep him quiet. Eric, sad to say, is blinkered in his attitudes. For my age I'm really very tough.'

She wheeled her chair to the alcove where the kettle and teapot stood on a tray, filled the pot and brought it to the table. A cat jumped on to the window sill and surveyed the scene with a pronounced smirk.

'Next door's moggy,' said Mrs Pledge. 'Good hunter. Keeps the vermin down.' She peered into the distance. 'Dear me,' she said, 'Eric seems to have tumbled into the moat.'

Tim was on his feet immediately, offering to go to the rescue.

'No, no,' said Mrs Pledge. 'Sit down, have your tea. Eric likes a swim. The dampness is probably not so beneficial for his arthritic joints but never mind. Poor Eric is starting to get a bit creaky.' She picked up the teapot. Large, ornate, with a picture of a bouncing hare on its side. 'Handsome, isn't it? I love hares. They make me think of spring. Now do you take sugar?'

'I've given it up,' said Tim.

The liquid trickled into his cup.

'Thick and treacly, just as it should be,' said Mrs Pledge. 'But it's not coming out very fast. There's some kind of blockage. A teabag must have got lodged in the spout.' She poked round with a spoon. 'That's more like it,' she said.

Tim lifted the cup to his lips. Mrs Pledge took a sip out of her own cup.

'So refreshing,' she said. 'What do you think?'

'It has a most distinctive flavour,' said Tim.

'I insist on the highest-quality teabags,' said Mrs Pledge. 'This is tea for the connoisseur, wouldn't you say?'

Tim emptied his cup in one lengthy gulp. 'It is the best tea I've ever tasted,' he said.

LIKE FATHER LIKE SON

MARGARET PELLING

It was one of those picture-perfect Oxford summer mornings. The air was full of greenness and flowery scents, the birds were twittering, the tourists hadn't begun to clog up Merton Street yet. Professor Giles Barrington noticed none of it as he made his way to the Examination Schools. But the lumbering run of an unfit man late for his own lecture yet again wasn't why his heart was pounding and his breath coming in gasps. It was the note he'd just had from his son. It was setting fire to his pocket.

Aha. Here was Dad, looking as pissed off as hell. He'd give himself a heart attack one of these days, running like that.

Robin Barrington smiled to himself as he ducked back up the side alley out of sight. Actually, maybe he should have stayed out in the street in full view of Dad: the baseball cap and hoodie was a pretty good disguise. On the other hand, how many hoodies did you ever see in Merton Street?

Robin's smile faded as he watched his father trundle up the street. What a sight. Hardly fifty, and he looked as if the undertakers would have to be called in soon. Faffing around with lectures and committees and stuff all the bloody time, and always, always late. No wonder he and Mum had nothing to say to each other these days. And to think how he was always going on about the academic life being so bloody marvellous.

Hm. Would Dad get the message this time? For a clever bloke he could be mighty thick.

'Oh, for goodness' sake!' said an annoyed female voice.

'Oh Christ, sorry!' said Giles, looking up, as two sets of notes, his and those of Dr Wendy Lowther, went cascading down the Exam Schools stairs. Half a dozen helpful undergraduates immediately started scrabbling for them, which meant that Wendy Lowther's notes and his own ended up jumbled together and had to be feverishly and frantically re-sorted.

'Sorry, sorry,' he mumbled, riffling through the pages. 'Not looking where I was going. Just had bad news.'

'Have you? I'm sorry,' she said, not looking at him. She didn't sound sorry.

As he offered her what looked like her share of the notes, he said, 'The least I can do is buy you a drink in the Bear tonight.'

'No thanks, I'm working,' said Wendy Lowther, still not looking at him. She all but snatched her notes out of his hand, and left him staring after her as she went on up the stairs, head high.

Oh God. All he'd wanted to do was tell nice, pretty Wendy Lowther about Robin, not give a Fellow of his own college the impression he was a dirty old man. Shit! He took a deep breath and hauled himself up the stairs to his own lecture room.

Half way through his lecture, Giles came to a sheet of notes which informed him that aristocratic women were active in land disputes throughout the later middle ages. One or two undergraduates in the front row looked up enquiringly as he ground to a halt. He blundered on, somehow, and nobody seemed all that disappointed when he finished telling them about Aspects of Greek History five minutes early.

He shuffled back to College, flopped down on his sofa, and pulled Robin's note out of his pocket. The words on it hadn't been miraculously transformed while he was lecturing. They said exactly what they'd said an hour ago:

Hi Dad,
Sorry, academic stuff and me just don't mix. I'm getting away for a while.
Seeya
Rob.

Giles reached for the phone and dialled home. Then he waited. And waited. Antonia surely couldn't be in the bloody studio at a time like this? Right. He'd go home and drag her out bodily to talk about their son if that was what it took.

It occurred to him that what he'd really wanted to tell

Wendy Lowther about was the whole damned mess that was his life. He had to tell somebody soon, or - or -

Or what, exactly? Bloody what?

Robin turned and pretended to be searching through his pockets for something as his dad cycled past. God, this was easy. The guy wouldn't have seen him if he'd stepped out in front of him and said 'Boo!'

He headed off down the street, making his way towards an address that people like Dad didn't know. He had a career to get on with, a career beyond Dad's wildest dreams.

'Antonia, I'm well aware that this latest commission is *gigantically* important,' said Giles, running his hands through what remained of his hair. 'But you must have some idea - what clothes are missing, did he take any money?'

'I haven't been into his room since he was ten, as you well know,' said the figure sitting at the kitchen table. Had she been like this when he married her: clay-stained jeans, black-rimmed fingernails, wild red hair? He should remember. He should care that he didn't remember.

'And as for money, he does have a bank account,' she went on, flicking the ash from her cigarette onto the floor. 'You fund it, Giles. He'll just have gone off for a day or so, OK? Cut him some slack, for fuck's sake.'

He stared again at the note Robin had left her, propped up against the empty wine bottle on the kitchen table:

Hi Mum,
Chilling out for a while, don't worry.
Love
Rob.

Just as eloquent as the note was Robin's mobile lying next to it. They could think again about phoning him.

'He'll be fine,' Antonia went on, pushing a strand of hair behind her ear. 'You fuss too much.'

'Fuss? Fuss?' shouted Giles. 'He's supposed to be doing his first A-level exam today!'

'All right, all right, he didn't want to. People do walk away from things. They do it all the time, Giles. Particularly if they're walking away from something Father decided is good for them.'

Giles's hands clenched and unclenched. To stop himself from applying them to her throat, he folded his arms tight and looked away from her. God, this kitchen. Dirty coffee cups everywhere, overflowing ash trays, plates of half-eaten food like some student flat. Could anybody blame him if one night a week sleeping in his college rooms after a function of some sort had become two nights, then three? If only he'd been here last night! If only he'd been here this morning!

'You're genuinely homeless?' said the man.

'Sure am, mate,' said Robin, slouching a bit more and toning down the nice-boy accent. 'Got chucked out the other day, like. I'm not doing drugs or nothin', just didn't see eye-to-eye.'

The man gave a shrug. 'Could I see your hostel receipt, please?'

Robin pulled out the piece of paper which would confirm where he'd been sleeping the last couple of nights, and handed it over. It seemed to do the trick. At any rate, the man gave him what he wanted.

Giles tried the police, who told him they couldn't treat Robin as missing, because of the notes he'd seen fit to leave. He went to Robin's school and saw the Headmaster, who said he'd talked to all Robin's friends and no one had any idea of where he'd gone.

On the way out of the school, all he saw were boys. This was hardly surprising in one of the top boys' schools in the country. But these were busy boys, dedicated boys, boys discussing the morning's exam with their friends. His son was brighter than any of them. The offer of a place at Oxford was the least surprising thing that had happened at this school in the past year, or any year for that matter.

On Magdalen Bridge Giles had to stop for a moment; this was all too much. He leaned on the parapet and looked down into the Cherwell, into the ranks of moored punts. There was a scrap of something pink in the bottom of one of them, floating in the bilge-water those punts tend to accumulate. A handkerchief? A pair of girl's knickers?

As he stood there, thirty years fell away from him in a tumbling heap. He was in a moored punt, not here but further up the Cherwell. There was a pair of knickers in the picture, and there was the girl - what had her name been? - who'd been wearing them but who wasn't any more. And there was him, Giles, two years older than Robin was now. Slim, golden-haired Giles Barrington, who'd just got the top first in Honour Moderations and who was heading for the top first in Finals.

Heading for where he was now. A Faculty Board meeting, late as ever.

Oh *hell*. He couldn't face it, he just couldn't. Let them improvise, let somebody else chair it for once, like that lazy bastard Donald Moorfoot. It was about time Moorfoot did a hand's turn around this university.

Giles put his head down and walked on until Rose Lane opened up on his left. A minute later he was in Christ Church Meadow. This felt odd to the point of weirdness. When was the last time he did something unexpected, out of order, downright irresponsible? The unsteadiness in his head seemed to be communicating itself to his feet, but he kept walking. He made his way down to Folly Bridge, where he got onto the Thames Path. He began to head upstream.

That day, Giles walked, and he walked. As one foot put itself in front of the other, the feeling that he was doing something dreadful, utterly beyond the pale, grew and grew. He followed the Thames Path out into the Oxfordshire countryside, but saw nothing. Then he came to a field of cows. One by one, they looked his way.

He turned and began to plod back the way he'd come. By the time he reached the outskirts of Oxford he was deathly tired and his stomach was caving in. Going in to College dinner and going home were equally out of the question, though. He went to McDonald's and bought a burger. While he was queuing to pay, he looked around him at an aspect of Oxford he knew nothing of. He might as well be in Peru.

A few yards away, a youth in a black T-shirt looked up,

and Giles's heart stopped. It was Robin.

The boy began to thread his way towards the door. As he came closer, it was clear he wasn't Robin. It wasn't only his face; Robin had a light, bouncing, agile, *intelligent* gait, he didn't shamble. Giles's eyes filled with tears, and he fumbled for his handkerchief.

Back in his college rooms, he bit into the burger. He got half way through it before he gagged and threw it in the bin.

Giles stayed in college, passing that night and several subsequent nights tossing and turning until the sky grew light. Each night, the pile of page proofs his publisher was on at him to look through grew higher. But he didn't want to go through the proofs of his latest book. He never wanted to see a page proof ever again. Why didn't he just stay in bed? Why didn't he lie there until the Bursar broke in and found his mouldering body?

Ah, hell. Each morning, he dragged himself out of bed, wincing and sighing, and made his customary furtive scamper into the shower at the bottom of the staircase. It wasn't something he relished, being noticed by students on his way to or from the shower. "Ageing don with dodgy marriage": he could see them thinking it.

Robin saw his father coming from fifty yards away. Christ, what a difference a week could make. He'd looked bad, now he looked the far side of terrible. Time for action.

As his dad shuffled closer, Robin cleared his throat. 'Buy the Big Issue, help the homeless,' he said as his dad drew level with him.

Dad looked up, frowning. He was evidently thinking this was another irritating Issue seller he was going to ignore - and then the jaw dropped open.

'*Robin?*' he said.

'Hi Dad,' said Robin.

'What in *hell* are you - '

'I'm almost done, let's go for coffee.'

Dad didn't move. 'Go for coffee? You've been missing a

week and you want to "go for *coffee*"?'

'Come on Dad. One of the places in the Market OK for you?' He took his father's shoulder and steered him down the street.

Giles stirred his coffee. 'It's not the money, Robin, I don't care about the squillions, as you put it, that I've paid out in school fees since you were four. I'm not thinking of you as an investment that's suddenly gone bad, for Christ's sake.'

'OK, but what about the like-father-like-son thing, though? I mean, there you are, son of Emeritus Professor Edgar Barrington, and here I am, son of Professor Giles Barrington - '

'Robin, I thought you'd find academic work *fun*.' Giles took a sip of coffee. He didn't meet Robin's eye. Maybe there was a bit of "like-father". But didn't all fathers want that, at some level?

Robin was laughing. 'Academe, fun? Look at you, Dad, just *look* at you.' Then the laughter stopped. Robin leaned towards him. 'I bet you're thinking, lucky sod, why haven't I done what he's done?'

'What? Oh, come on!' Giles took another swig of coffee. Ridiculous notion! So ridiculous that he was getting a shifting sensation under his solar plexus. 'Look, when are you coming home?'

Robin looked down, into his coffee. 'Dunno,' he said at last. 'I'm not just selling the Issue, you know, I'm washing up in a night shelter. I'm getting to know some people. Interesting people. And before you ask, I'm not taking drugs.'

'But where are you living, for God's sake?'

'Oh, here and there. I'm doing the right thing, Dad, trust me. I've been saying Oxford's not for me ever since I got in, and I meant it.'

But I thought all that was teenage posturing. Giles couldn't say it. Not now.

Robin downed the last of his coffee and got to his feet. 'Thanks, Dad. I'll be in touch,' he said, and went off in the direction of the High Street.

Giles stayed sitting there for a minute or so longer, gazing at the dregs of his own coffee. Then he went out through the Covered Market the way Robin had gone.

He stood at the Market entrance for a few moments, looking up and down the High Street. There was no sign of Robin. He started walking. Where had he been going before he ran into Robin? He couldn't remember.

After he had wandered aimlessly for what felt like hours, his eye was caught by a poster in a travel agent's window. Cloud-capped mountains rose behind a plateau covered with ancient ruins. Superimposed on the scene were a smiling dark-haired woman and a child, dressed in brightly coloured hats and jackets. "Peru, Land of Contrasts" was blazoned along the top of the poster.

Giles looked at the poster for maybe a minute, then went into the shop. 'A ticket to Peru, please,' he said. 'For tomorrow.'

'Tomorrow?' The assistant frowned. 'I don't think there'll be anything available at this short notice, sir.'

'Please try.'

There was a cancellation on a flight leaving at six a.m. Giles took it.

Outside the shop, Robin smiled as he looked through the window. Then, before his father turned away from the counter, he crossed the street and disappeared into the crowd.

OGGI

CHRIS BLOUNT

I hadn't seen Oggi for several years; certainly he hadn't been in the Oxford Night Shelter since it had been rebuilt. Oggi didn't like the Shelter, in fact he didn't like Oxford at all; he hated most towns, though he could tolerate villages, at least those which had not been spoiled by what he called "them smarties".

I had first met Oggi when I worked in the shelter as a volunteer in 1993. It was fairly grim in those days, with lots of unsavoury characters who were very violent and very drunk. Now everyone has their own room, and even Oggi acknowledged the huge improvement in the accommodation. The night I saw him was bitterly cold, just as it was when I had first met him all those years ago: very, very cold, certainly too cold for Oggi to sleep rough, though he had walked all the way to Oxford from Wallingford.

As a young man, Oggi had been a chair bodger; they worked and lived in the great beech woods near High Wycombe, and their craft greatly contributed to that town's reputation as the centre of England's furniture manufacturing industry. Some say that the chair bodgers ceased work in the late 1950s, but I bought a set of beautiful hand-made Windsor chairs from the men in the woods in 1976.

I don't know why Oggi left Buckinghamshire around that time and moved west to Oxfordshire. He has never told me and I have never asked; all I know is that he has never crossed the border back to the "leafy county" ever since.

Oggi was more than a bodger; he was a real countryman. Oxfordshire became his adopted county and he knew every byway from Banbury (though he would never admit to going there) to Shiplake, and from Burford to Thame. Oggi made his living doing odd jobs, mainly gardening, carpentry, and fencing. He had known some of his clients for forty years, but like him, they were getting older; some had died, some had moved to smaller houses with only tiny gardens and some had even moved into flats, so Oggi's "client base" and his source of income was drying up.

Even so, it wasn't a bad life; there was a small core of "gaffers" who would always find work for him in the winter if there was no gardening work. One or two even asked him to house-sit while on their winter holidays, knowing it would be somewhere warm for Oggi, and reassured that the house was occupied. They would let him bring Cuff, his old collie; Cuff would never sleep in the house but Oggi would always find him a garden shed.

'Hello Mr B, how are you?'

'Oggi - it's a really long time since you've been to see us. Are you OK?'

'Tell the truth, Mr B, I'm not too good, and nor is Cuff: he really feels the cold now, and, you know, the last few nights... So now you take dogs, I thought I'd come in... and I got to see the docs next door, not that I really believe 'em. Not sure how Cuff will get on with that shepherd cross, mark you, but now we each got our own rooms, shouldn't be a problem; Cuff'll be delighted.'

'So what's wrong, Oggi? Nothing serious, I hope.'

'Well... can we go somewhere quiet?'

Oggi had been working the woods around Maidensgrove the previous summer; he had been asked by one of his oldest "gentlemen" to make four Windsor chairs. The practising bodgers used to have proper workshops in the woods; they had their own homes and were not itinerant like Oggi. They were very skilled pole-lathe turners, a craft which Oggi had mastered but which he had not used for many years.

The old craftsmen would bid for "stands" or parcels of standing timber every autumn. When the Oxfordshire estates thinned their beech woods, they often left the standing timber for several months. Oggi knew of several stacks around the south of the county, and knew how much timber he would need for four Windsors. The problem was how to transport it; he planned to take a few pieces from each of five stacks, but the stacks were a few miles apart and his client lived another few miles up the county towards Thame.

Obtaining a horse and cart would be too suspicious and he certainly wasn't going to trust the travellers who had a site nearby; neither did he want to involve his client, who might well consider that the raw materials had been appropriated dishonestly. Oggi's view was that once the timber had been "stacked" for over a season, and not taken, he earned "woodman's rights". As a bodger in his early days, he would have been horrified to think he would ever reach that conclusion: but times were very hard.

'Thing is, Mr B, I'm in a spot of bother. I was trying to move some timber the other day and half the pile fell on my foot. Think I've broken something. Hurts like someone sticking needles in me and it doesn't help that I walked from Wallingford 'cos they threw us off the bus when some bloody woman saw poor old Cuff was bleeding from his leg... and I had to bloody carry him. I think I should go to the vet myself, rather than them doctors.'

I took him to the nurse, who cleaned up both man and dog and gave them some painkillers. Afterwards, they sat quietly in the corner, eating supper, but not mixing with the other residents. They were gone the next morning. Later I heard that Cuff was picked on that night by the shepherd cross; the surgery had put him down, as Oggi couldn't afford to pay for the vet. He must have been devastated; that dog was the only living thing he loved, as far as I knew.

But he left me a note, asking me to meet him in an old woodland pub, the Black Horse at Checkendon. This pub, long since modernised, at that time only opened for irregular hours at the discretion of the landlady. So several weeks later, at 6.30 on a cold February night, Oggi and I were the only customers, each nursing a pint of Brakspear's, when he told me the rest of his story. He was too proud to show his feelings about Cuff.

'There were two stacks left, close to each other, in the same wood. I had to work with Billy. I never trusted him, but I had no choice, 'cos I don't drive and he had this old van, see. Bloody sure, he don't have a licence, but still we couldn't have done it without that van.

'I had roped the last part of the stack nearest the road, and Billy had taken the van into the middle of the wood. Funny thing was, I thought I heard voices from that direction, which got me worried as I didn't want nobody to see the stacks being loaded. So I'd thought I'd stay where I was, 'cos they'd only have seen Billy moving 'em.

'After a bit, the voices stopped and I heard him switch on the van and move off. I was waiting for him to come back. Then I thought I heard him get stuck in the mud, and then I heard nothing. But he must have driven out the wood the other way, which is real steep and bloody difficult 'specially with a full load of timber. So all I could do with my stack was nothing except leave it and hobble home.

'I reckon Billy took his cut on the chairs I was making from the wood. Now Billy and I go back a long way, 'cos both of us got thrown out of Bucks at the same time for the same reason, but I've never really trusted him. I was going to give him a cut on the chairs I was making after we had all the timber, but he must have reckoned he'd take his profit there and then. Anyroad, so he's nicked the last bit of my timber' - the irony clearly eluded Oggi - 'and I've only enough for three Windsors.'

'Look, Oggi,' I said, 'I don't mind lending you some money to buy some timber from a yard, but I'm not getting involved with taking stacked wood.'

'No, Mr B, I'm not asking that; I've already covered that. The man I'm making 'em for will lend me the cash and is happy to wait a few months. I told him I can't make 'em for a bit on account of my leg, see.' Oggi proudly showed me his plaster. 'Your nurse told me I had to go the docs next door to the shelter. Yeah, very good they are. Never asked how it happened or anything. Tendons or something and the ankle's bust, but it'll all be OK - be walkin' from here to Oxford again by May!'

There were still no other customers and I could feel Oggi getting uncomfortable, so I ordered another couple of pints. Oggi cleared his throat and pulled out a packet of Drum, ready to roll his own in a green Rizla. Smoking indoors in pubs was still legal for the moment, though I couldn't see Oggi or the landlady following the rules even after 1st July.

Then two customers, one of whom I knew was a local farmer, came into the pub. We nodded recognition to each other. The man I acknowledged also seemed to know Oggi; his brow furrowed briefly before he returned to the deep conversation with his friend. Oggi went very quiet, got up to find the Gents, and, on returning, made an excuse about going home before it snowed, and left, despite my offer of a lift.

It was another few weeks before I heard from Oggi again, via a handwritten note at the Luther Street Medical Centre. Oggi did not "do" phones, and left no way of contacting him, so I had little choice but to meet him at the King William in Hailey, near Ipsden, again at 6.30 on a midweek evening, as he had specified. I was keen to find out what had prompted him to leave so suddenly at our last meeting.

The King William is a popular and tastefully converted pub, which serves good food, but it seemed an improbable location for Oggi to choose. I would have thought it would be full of the sort of people he despised, and was not convinced he would turn up. But he was there and seemed very pleased to see me. In fact he had already bought me a pint.

He spoke very quietly: he had been up to the spot in Greenfield Wood where he had buried Cuff; and had found a carved inscription on the beech tree, which overlooked the grave, just a few yards from the stack which Oggi had "used" for the chairs.

He insisted on showing it to me that night, even though it was by now pitch dark. To my surprise, Oggi had ridden to the pub on a moped, which we loaded into the car. I asked him why he was so keen to show me now and why he had left so suddenly in the Black Horse. He simply put his finger to his lips and said, 'Later.'

We left the car at the Five Horseshoes in Maidensgrove; this pub was already quite full, as it too had a good reputation for food, and Oggi clearly did not want to be seen there. From the car park, it was possible to climb over a fence round the back of a few cottages and follow a track into the woods behind Russells Water. From there we crossed the Henley road and went into Greenfield Wood.

We both had torches and Oggi, leading the way, seemed to have the eyesight of a deer, but I fell over several times before we reached the clearing. It was probably the most secluded spot you could find in the whole of the south of England.

The carving had faded, but the letters OGGI were clear. I couldn't decipher the rest of the inscription: it looked like a very poorly drawn heart with an arrow through it. Oggi thought the arrow was a seven and the heart was a five.

'Oggi, have you broken some poor girl's heart?' I teased him: he didn't reply.

Later, in the Rising Sun at Witheridge Hill, he told me the rest of the story.

'Billy and I left Bucks because of a girl, Emilia. We were both seeing her. She was a bodger's daughter and her mother was Italian. Emilia called me Oggi, and her name for Billy was Domani. She got in the family way, but neither of us knew which one... ' Oggi was clearly very unhappy to be revealing this. 'Her father told us both to leave the area and never return. We heard that Emilia had a daughter but she was only sixteen and her father made her have the baby adopted. A few months ago, I had to go into Henley for one of my old ladies: she's in a bad way, see, and can't get out and her housekeeper was away for the day. So I go to this posh food shop that sells foreign cheese and sausages and that, and I walk up and down outside working out how to say what she's asked for, see; and then I see her.'

I looked puzzled.

'Yeah, I'm sure it's her, Emilia, only she's older like, but very... well, still very pretty.' Oggi blushed like a young lad on his first date. 'And I thought, she won't remember me, and even if she does, well, she won't want to know me. And then I thought about how we used to "arrange" things with her. She used to pretend she was teaching us Italian; so if I went up to see her in her father's workshop, I would say

"Signorina, formaggio per favore", and she would laugh and say "Si Oggi", or... '

'Or what?' I asked.

'So anyway, I went into the shop, and she looked up and she knew who I was, and I said "Signorina, formaggio per favore". She looked proper upset and turned away and covered her face with her hands.

'I waited a bit, and was about to leave, when she turned round and said, "No, no Domani!" And when she spoke, I knew who'd been talking to Billy in the wood.'

Oggi kept saying, 'Thank you, Mr B, for listening; I've never told anyone before.' He insisted on buying me another pint.

While he was at the bar, I was doodling with the inscription with the heart and the arrow in front of OGGI, or the possibility that it could be a five and a seven.

'Oggi, swallow that pint quickly; we're off to Henley.'

He looked completely baffled, but now it was my turn to insist. I knew exactly where the deli was, and I pulled up right outside.

'There's your answer; she's been looking for you. Look at the phone number on the shop door. Your Emilia's a clever girl, and you're right, it is a five and a seven. All Henley numbers start with 57 and for OGGI, you can also read 0661, so there you are, 570661: "OGGI, my heart is broken but, you can find me on 570661".'

One thing still puzzled me. 'Oggi, why were you so worried about the man in the Black Horse?'

Oggi was still reeling with the discovery of his old love: but he muttered, 'He's the man I'm making the Windsors for!'

BURNING WORDS

JANE STEMP

There were sparrows in the dust below, scuffling over a chance ear of wheat fallen from a load of fodder. Petronilla knelt on the window seat and pressed close to the diamond panes so that she could watch them.

It was a bright, cold day, with a bitter wind scudding rags of clouds across the sky. A flock of students, gowns flapping like crows' wings, ran out from where the Turl cut the city wall, then along Canditch towards Balliol College. One was struggling to keep his cap on over his pale hair, and when a book slipped from under his arm and bowled into the ditch itself, he never seemed to notice, but ran on under the college gateway as if he were already late.

Petronilla glanced at the baby, sound asleep, in her care until her mother had finished arguing with the cook downstairs. There were fifteen years, and too many child-ghosts, between Petronilla and Thomas, but she was glad of him. He was more than a year old now: an heir for the shop and trade in spices, and healthy enough to take some of the weight of their father's hopes from her shoulders. And at last their mother, who had seemed smaller and paler with every passing year, was in good heart and health again. Even at her frailest she had been able to stand up to the cook and the maidservant together, so she would be a long time in the kitchen.

The book would most likely be in Latin - after all, it belonged to a student - but in this year of grace 1555 there were books in English. Petronilla could read English, because when she had been heir to the shop her father had made sure that she was taught her letters; but she owned no books. And she had always wanted one book to call her own, whether she could read it or not.

Without thinking about it any more, she picked up her skirts and ran soft-footed downstairs, through the shop pungent with spices, into the street, under Northgate and along outside the row of houses against the city wall, on the edge of Canditch.

The worst thing about the book's having fallen where it had was that she had to pass the burned ground. On this windy day it was swirling with ash, and she lifted the hem of her skirts still higher. There was the book, on the edge of the ditch and not fallen deep in. With a slight gasp she stepped down, picked it up, and ran home.

The parlour, and the baby, were quiet. Petronilla sat down and opened the book at random. It was in English, and she read, her lips moving slightly. Then she clapped the book shut, shivering. Opened it again, as if it might be different: but it wasn't.

She had been seven when King Henry had died and Edward had come to the throne. She could just remember her parents grumbling, later, about the new English prayer book, and buying one for show when visitors came. Then, after Edward died and Queen Mary was crowned, her mother put the prayer book away and set out the shrine of the Virgin with its candle once more. But that was all.

And this book, between her hands, was heresy, or maybe treason - or both - and she knew so little about either: but enough to be afraid. On the title page was written, in a crabbed hand, "To my good friend Edward Marchant, with all blessing, Hugh L" - there was a surname, too, but she would not decipher it, not now, when the reek of ash suddenly blew into the room as the wind sent the smoke back down the chimney. She stared at the floor, at her feet, anywhere but out of the window.

For all the care she had taken, her skirts were black at the hem. Yet it was weeks since the fire had burned in the ditch, and autumn had passed to a cold, dry winter. People had taken pinches of the ash away, secretly, but it seemed that the dark circle would be there forever. She had been in the house that day, when the fire burned, but not in this room with the sunshine and the view of the Canditch. She had stayed downstairs, trying to ignore everything, the noise, the crowd, especially the smell. Pepper, cloves, cinnamon, galingale: despite everything in the shop, the smell had been overwhelming. Even now, sometimes, it made her sick to smell meat roasting.

She opened the book again. She had to read that name. "With all blessing, Hugh Latimer."

Hugh Latimer, who was now no more than ash blowing in

the street, and charred bone.

Her hands closed round the leather binding. The book was not so very large, but difficult to hide in the room she shared with the maidservant, and too dangerous to keep. Unless - and then Thomas began to cry. Petronilla knotted the book into her shift, safe under gown and kirtle and petticoat, and all the rest of the day as she went about her duties felt it tapping on her knees: a reminder, a threat, a bad conscience nagging. She slept badly, the book under her pillow, and woke out of nightmares when Jonnet the maidservant opened the shutters, which always creaked. She had to be up betimes to bake the morning bread, and was gone before Petronilla could greet her.

The sky was grey as the frost on the windowsill. In the dawn twilight Petronilla saw, not sparrows this morning, but two students out in the road, pacing across it and back, looking, looking, and she knew what for. She began to dress.

'Face the truth, Ned.' The voice drifted up to her, kindly but with a sharp edge. 'It's been swept up with the horse-muck and carted away to someone's field. You'll not find it again.'

The other stopped short, put both hands to his head and ran them back so that the pale hair she had noticed yesterday stood up like a furze-bush between his fingers. 'Well enough, Hal. I'll believe you. Twice more across, and then to breakfast. But if anyone finds it, and it a gift from him, with my name in - '

'Your father's name.'

'The same.'

Petronilla took the book from under her pillow, leaned out, and moved one shutter. It creaked, and two faces turned towards her. She lifted the book. Ned stretched out cupped hands as if she held him on puppet-strings; Hal, taller and darker, mouthed, 'Go on!'

The shutter was not the only thing in the house that creaked: the top stair gave just enough warning of someone climbing to the garret. Petronilla spun away from the window, pushed the book under her mattress, and was shaking the pillow when her mother came in to the room with Thomas on one arm.

'Ah, good child, you're out of bed.'

Petronilla did not feel good: she felt as if she was caught

on a whirligig of wickedness. She wanted to blot out the remembered fear in Ned's voice, she wanted to help, but his name and Hugh Latimer's seemed to burn through the mattress like flame, hanging in the air. She laid down the pillow and said, clearly, aware of the open shutter behind her, 'I thought I might go to Mass, at St Michael's.' And curtsied. 'If it please you, Mother.'

'It pleases me very well,' her mother said, smiling. 'I trust you not to linger there, my child.' She turned away, cooing at Thomas, and did not see Petronilla's answering smile grow too stiff to stay on her face.

Before she left the house Petronilla said a Hail Mary in front of the little shrine, partly because she always did, but also because she had never felt more in need of protection. The wind gusted in when she opened the door, making the candle flicker and blowing a loose curl across her face. Outside, she tucked her hair firmly under her coif again, and picked her way along the Cornmarket, one hand holding her cloak at the front.

She was early at the church. Inside, in the angle between the south wall and the west, she knelt, and put her hands over her face as if she were praying. Under her cloak was a linen kerchief, and in that was the book: which was, after all, something to pray about.

Presently someone knelt beside her. She risked a glance over the top of her fingers. It was Hal, not even pretending to pray, but sitting back on his heels. Nor was he wearing his student's gown. His doublet and hose were appropriately sombre, but she thought his cloak was velvet. One hand rested on a bejewelled cap with a feather, the other on a book wrapped in gold-embroidered cloth. He moved nearer. 'What's your name, little mistress?'

'Petronilla.'

'Just Petronilla?'

'Yes,' she said. 'The other is no business of yours.'

She was answered by a soft chuckle. 'So much for the pious child who asks leave to go to Mass!'

'You know why,' she said.

'I do. And I thank you.' His voice was kind, as she had heard it outside her window, but when he spoke again there was that same sharp edge to it. 'Ned's a good friend, and a better scholar than I'll ever be, but he's going the right way to get himself roasted if he doesn't take care.'

'Oh, don't,' she said, and buried her face in her hands again. 'Why do people do such things?'

The church was filling. 'Stand up for what they believe in?' Hal said, still hard-voiced, but quietly.

'No. Burn the ones who do.'

'Ah.' He sighed. 'That I don't know. Do you have the book?'

She slid it from under the edge of her cloak, and he reached across and took it, all in one swift movement that nobody could have seen who hadn't been watching: but although the church was full now, they were at the back, behind everyone else.

Throughout the Mass Petronilla knelt and stood and did what was needed as if someone else was moving her body. Beside her Hal was doing the same, his book open, but always at the same place. If she raised her eyes she could see half of one page: Latin, and the corner of a picture, feet and folds of cloth and black-lined tufts of grass.

Afterwards, when they were alone again, Petronilla sat on the stone bench and said, 'Where's Ned - Edward?'

'Biting his nails through a class on Aristotle,' Hal answered, sitting down beside her. 'I should be there too, but nobody shouts if *I* miss a lecture. Besides, it's safer this way.'

The stone was cold and hard on her right: he was warm on the other. 'What will you do with the book?' she asked.

He shook it out of her kerchief. 'To begin with, this.' The title page ripped out, a sharp noise like an indrawn breath. Hal turned the book over, and opened it at the last page, blank except for a printed device and some few words. 'Now this.' Another rip. 'And I'll find some innocent title for Ned to paste in the front, and maybe rebind it, and all's safe. They never read farther than the front page and the back.' He handed the two loose pages back to her. 'Will you burn these for me when you get home - Petronilla?'

The church was silent now, and deserted. It smelt, faintly, of stale incense and beeswax candles. Not of burning. She took the pages, and rolled them in her kerchief. 'Yes.'

'And,' Hal said, 'will you answer me a question?'

Petronilla looked at him.

'Why did you pick up Ned's book?'

'I was looking at the sparrows,' she said, 'and I saw Ned - Edward - drop it, and - '

'Not a sparrow falls... or a book. And?' Hal prompted.

'I always wanted a book of my own. Any book.'

'Ah.'

'I ran out of the house and past here and out of the gate, and I was afraid... ' She stopped.

'Afraid someone might see you?'

'Of the ash. Of the burning.'

He was very still. For a long moment he said nothing. And then, 'What do you believe?'

'I believe books are important.' She wound her hands in her cloak. 'What about you?'

'I believe people are more important.'

'Even than the truth?'

'Sometimes.' He pulled off the gold-embroidered cover from his book, and fitted it over Ned's. 'Perhaps you'd like this.' And he held out to her his own book.

'But - I can't - and Mother would ask - '

'And you would tell the truth. I see.' He stood up, and put on his cap. 'Tell her that you found it in the church, then. Or outside. And that nobody came back for it. Because that will be true.' Hal opened the door; he was a plumed and cloaked shadow against the light. Gently he dropped his book on the exact centre of the threshold, and was gone.

'I LOVED YOU'

RAY PEIRSON

I don't work the night shift any more.

They all think they know why, but they are wrong. The office gossips, men just as malicious as the women, won't say anything to my face, but conversations still fade as I enter the canteen at lunch-time.

The managers take a sympathetic line. Time is a great healer, they say, and pretend not to have heard the office gossip. Very sensible, too. Kate's husband still works in Accounts and my wife Susie is the popular star of Software Sales.

I try to avoid thinking about it. I've stopped smoking. I've started on a strict diet; no more toffees. I've taken up Salsa. My new little boat is moored down on the Thames. I even cry a little in between all these fun things. I spend a few moments every day wondering if Susie really knows. Not all of it, obviously, but she has been so sympathetic and understanding that I think she must. But every night before the sleeping pill pulls me down, I'm back there.

It was a night like any other. In the sort of office block any office worker would cheerfully die for. Five years before, the company had relocated from London. They had converted a listed building in North Oxford and crammed it full of computers. You will remember the uproar in Academic Oxford. Another lost cause. The various ghosts that were supposed to haunt the old structure added character and price. It had won design awards because the computer bits failed to spoil the elegance of the original building. The central courtyard became a green oasis of fashionable atrium and that was the view from my desk. I was well-placed to watch most of the departments at work. Computers are my work but people are my interest.

I even watched for the ghosts walking. Just to pass the time, you understand, though the house had retained an atmosphere in which ghosts ridiculously seemed all too possible. Especially after office parties with the usual jokes about spirits. Computers are... well, dead boring. The rumours of ghosts in the old house had fuelled all the talk but maybe, regretfully, the micro-chips had frozen them all out.

Luckily I was very seldom exposed to such time-wasting stuff; the solitary night shift hours protected me. All the same, the older parts of the building emptied quickly after dark.

As usual that night, I took over from Jack. He grunted some friendly obscenity and vanished without giving me a proper briefing. Situation normal. He was like that. Perhaps all computer operators are odd. Perhaps I'm odd too, but if so I have the politeness to take a job which gives me scope for oddness without upsetting other people.

I have my little foibles. I change the coffee machine cartridge to Kenyan. I check all the computer monitors in order, left to right. I put my fresh bag of forbidden toffees in the half-open drawer for quick closure just in case of a snap inspection. Sticky toffees and computer servers in a dust-free environment don't mix. There are exactly 16 toffees in every pack. One for every half hour of my night shift as a self-important but very lonely Operations Controller. My little kingdom is now nearly complete.

But not quite. There is one final item. Sometimes the high spot of my day, or rather night. Across the small central atrium I can see into the programming suite. Programmers aren't allowed into the operations section. Fraud is much easier if you can actually handle the tapes and disks. So programmers live in a different world from operators like myself and might as well be on the moon.

Maybe being unattainable makes the ladies more desirable. Grass is greener, if they have grass on the moon. That is how it started. The night she started. I could see the suggestion of movement and the flickering shadow of a woman under the fluorescent lighting. I had been to the leaving-do the previous day so was ready to look over the new lady. Like when you wait to see the new registration number on cars in March and September. Or at least I do.

Kate leaned round her console and we stared for what

seemed forever. She was not everybody's cup of tea but she was my cup of tea. Each night thereafter I watched her slender hands carefully arranging her bits and pieces and her shadow flickering on the wall. Until one night I spotted what could only be a bag of toffees moving quickly across and down out of sight. The next night, or rather early morning at the end of the night shift, I parked my car beside her red Fiesta in the office car park. In a cold dawn we met. We sat in her car behind the frosty windscreen for hours, just talking and eating toffees. I actually saw my wife drive in to start her day.

This became a habit until one morning, after the bag of toffees was empty, and our conversation had faltered to a halt, I invited her home for breakfast. If we had been hungry, not so many toffees in the bag you understand, we would, I think, have been all right. But we had lost our appetite for food.

It was absurdly easy. We would spend the nights together in total innocence, physically if not mentally, glancing occasionally at each other across the courtyard. Peek-a-boo round the consoles. She was hidden by the terminals most of the time, but I knew she was there. The flicker of a shadow on the wall behind her, the movement of a file from desk to cupboard with only the pink of her hands visible. Just knowing, really, she was there. My life transformed in the dry hum and electronic double-talk of the big mainframes. A toffee and a shared smile; my working life.

And although we were separated by locked doors and an atrium, we could talk endlessly on the private company net. Her "I love you" would come up on the screen in a different colour every evening. I guess it is a commonplace that men find it difficult to say "I love you" except in the extremis of proposals or, more cynically, propositions. But for once, in the cosy world of my terminal meeting hers in electronic embrace, my "I love you" could be typed out effortlessly.

I don't need to go into all that. Other people's love-talk comes across pretty gooey. And pretty tedious to onlookers. But we canoodled electronically all night, digital pillow-talk if you like, and the night shift became a hotbed of virtual sensuality.

I don't know what set it off. Yes, I do really. It had become such a comfortable habit spending our days together. We would play for safety from discovery by watching my wife arrive for her day at the office. I know, I know. Not very nice! But adultery is nothing new in this tired old world. And don't get me wrong. I loved my wife. As well. Even if I found it difficult to say the words out loud.

Kate and I would make love in the dawn as usual and have our usual companionable breakfast together. She had taken to Kenyan coffee and had switched me to a healthy cereal, rather than my usual fry-up. We shared the crossword; something I could never do with my wife.

Two left feet. I think I must have two left feet both placed firmly in my mouth.

'This is a wonderful routine,' I said across the kitchen table. 'Two attractive women to cook for me. Breakfast and love in the morning with you, darling Kate. Dinner and love in the evening with wife Susie. What more can a man ask for?'

The cereal bowls Kate was carrying across to the sink smashed on the tiled kitchen floor. I rushed to help clean up. 'Don't,' she screamed. This was more shocking than the sudden smash. She was crying. I stood there like a man does, looking sympathetic, but blank. Afraid to say the wrong words, unable to think of any right ones.

I don't want to dwell on the next two hours. Surely Kate enjoyed our little routine as well? Why spoil things? How could I tell Susie? Did she really want to upset Susie? How could I leave Susie? I love Susie. Well, we got on, anyway, I said. She was my wife. We had a big mortgage. She would be terribly upset.

These were not the right words. The coffee mugs went as well. Kenyan is dark and sticky. It took forever to clean up. I stammered out the usual stuff. I hadn't realised she felt as strongly as... and I did, well, love her. Hadn't I typed it often enough? And what about her husband? If we went on as we were, nobody would be... Not the right answer. We parted. She was very white and did not kiss me goodbye.

The day was not the happiest one. It stretched endlessly. Deep down I was scared. I was settled nicely in my little world. Kate wanted me to jump ship and start again. Terribly flattering, very exciting, but very, very scary. Was it possible to love two? I didn't know, but the guilt flowed endlessly.

I cooked tea for Susie when she arrived home full of her day at six o'clock. She was bursting with an office scandal, related with great relish. I tried to show the right sort of interest but the sudden fear of my involvement in the very next scandal left me trembling. The romantic frisson of the goings-on had left her in the right sort of mood for love. If you are on the night shift you have to grab opportunities as they arise. I did my best and left for work leaving a pink but thoughtful Susie watching TV on the set in the bedroom.

I had dragged my feet a little in getting ready. On the night shift, everything is topsy-turvy, but I shaved closely and dressed more carefully than usual. I took my time, with my mind off-line. I was suddenly, unforgivably, late. Computers cannot wait. The data comes down the cable, bounces off satellites, you name it, with a schedule timed to the nano-second. And I was late.

In the end I drove hurriedly towards the office in the dark of a heavy rainstorm that matched my mood. Starting late as I had, I was furious at the sudden delay in my short-cut through the town. The traffic flash on Radio Oxford told me about the accident, but as usual, too late and only seconds before the blue flashing lights on the Abingdon Road stopped me dead. Somebody else who had been in too much of a hurry. It might easily have been me, in my upset state. I sat in the traffic queue pondering on mortality.

For moments I hoped that I might squeeze past, but the almost unrecognisable wreckage of a car blocked the road, and it was no go. It had to be an infuriatingly long diversion round the ring road, making me later still. An ambulance sirened past me on the wrong side, from the direction of the accident, travelling very quickly towards the John Radcliffe. From the urgency I guessed some poor devil was in a very bad way. I wished them well.

I was fifteen unforgivable minutes late; computer

schedules waiting for no man. Or woman! Kate was even later: her car was not in its usual place. Probably delayed by the same accident, I decided. It was directly on her usual route.

Jack was furious; somehow this cancelled out my own mood. I looked across at Kate's window. Even in the flurry of catch-up work, I was a bit puzzled. Despite the absence of her car, her shadow was already flickering faintly on the wall behind her terminal. What with rows and diversions, and key employees late, the company was really out of luck tonight.

I leaned forward so she could look across and see my wave. Tonight she was playing hard to get, staying out of sight behind her terminal. I shrugged. Women! She would get over it after a while. Common sense, it was only common sense, to continue as we were. Why hurt other people. I did... well, love her. Of course I did. But there was Susie! We had been through a lot together.

I was thinking such fatuous male thoughts but really I was waiting, playing for time. Waiting for her words to come up on the screen. What colour would she program tonight? Given her mood, perhaps it would be a red "I love you". Scarlet, even. A sort of "I love you but I'm furious" female mixed message.

I waited. And waited. I had to do something to break the deadlock. I was suddenly scared. Would she try to end it all? The hum of the machines and the electric blue of the anti-static carpets suddenly seemed less cosy. The tube lighting was harsh and unforgiving. And what if our affaire got out and I lost Susie as well as Kate? An abyss yawned beneath me.

I decided for once to begin our dialogue myself.

I looked again across the courtyard. Her shadow, now curiously faded, was still there. And was that her bag of toffees? I typed some words. Tentative at first. I'm a man! I paused for an acknowledgement but none came. The dam broke. I flooded the screen with words that had been held back that morning.

Now all I could do was to wait. I had committed myself. I felt warm and cold at the same time. Minutes stretched and tears came to my eyes. Was this the end?

And then the words came slowly. As though she hadn't read my impassioned outburst. As though I hadn't reached her even though she was within yards. Not a reply, just an aloof statement from far away.

'I loved you.'

I cried. Was she saying it was over? The studied use of the past tense was absolute. The colour was odd. Not scarlet as of anger, not blue as of sadness. In fact not really any colour, just sort of pale, almost transparent, and difficult to see. I typed some more words but my hope was fading. This seemed so final. You don't miss someone so badly until they are gone. I became convinced she was cutting communications for good.

And then those words once more.

Their colour had faded so I had to angle my head to see past the reflections on the screen. I looked across the courtyard, just in case I could signal. Even her shadow was no longer there. Perhaps she really had walked out. Even as the idea crystallised I realised, how silly. The company's computer schedule was far too important.

Despite the practicalities, without knowing how exactly, I knew deep inside I had lost her. There was a sort of emptiness, where previously she had made herself at home. Without much hope I went out into the dawn to try one last time by her car.

The car park was still empty.

You know the rest. I attended the funeral. Not to do so would have looked odd. Everybody watched my face. I tried to contain my grief. They had all known. It was obvious.

Later, unaccountably, I became more cheerful, despite still missing Kate in the here and now. I felt privileged. I even went back to toffees for a while. But somehow I could not go back to my beloved night shift. I was deathly afraid of the emptiness now that she was gone. And deathly afraid that the flickering shadow might return. Or not return.

I said nothing to anyone about that night. I was comforted by her final words.

Words that she could not leave without saying.

'I loved you.'

THE BODLEIAN MURDERS

LINORA LAWRENCE

The Bodleian Library has stood on its present site since 1602, Bodley's Librarian succeeding Bodley's Librarian in an orderly and proper fashion until 1985, when the then incumbent of the post announced his retirement at the end of the year. What followed was anything but orderly and proper.

D.I. Kris Lipinski had a degree from Bristol University, but Oxford academics would think nothing of that - they probably had two of those for breakfast every morning. Moving on to the non-Oxbridge universities for lunch, with Yale and Harvard for dinner. What would they have for afternoon tea? An Adult Education Course in the History of Art, perhaps?

'I must stop doing this!' Kris muttered to himself as he strode over to his car. 'It's displacement activity!' He inserted his keys in the lock just as his colleague arrived, and motioned to her to get in.

'Ever been to the Bodleian Library?' he asked, easing his vehicle out of the police-station car park into the Oxford traffic.

'You're kidding, aren't you?' Sergeant Jessima Banerji replied. 'Why would I go there?'

Kris regarded her: newly assigned to him, attractive, smart, ambitious and straight from South London. What was she going to make of the Oxford scene?

'Try not to be too anti,' he suggested. 'It's only part of what Oxford's all about. Anyway, they have a suspicious death on their hands, so they're the same as anyone else as far as I'm concerned.'

They parked in Catte Street and announced their arrival to an agitated porter on duty at the Great Gate. 'Yes, I'll ring Dr de Bok immediately. He'll come right out.'

Moments later an old, carved wooden door, with the words Schola Metaphysicae painted on the stone above, opened, and Dr Julius de Bok, Secretary of the Library, strode across the quadrangle. He was a middle-aged, fair-haired man with a confident handshake.

'I thought we would be meeting Bodley's Librarian,' said Kris.

'Well, being Secretary of the Library means I am the chief administrator, bit like being the Dean of a Cathedral, so this unfortunate business comes under my remit, really.'

'But if there was a murder in a cathedral, surely the Bishop would get involved?'

'Well, to be honest, Dr Fadden isn't here yet,' admitted de Bok. 'It's still quite early by his standards. Shall I take you to see the body?'

'That's the general idea,' said Kris. 'I take it nothing has been touched or moved?'

'No, indeed not.' De Bok led Kris and Jessima towards the Divinity School and then to a door in one corner of the Proscholium, which he unlocked, using a set of master keys. 'I've posted two porters to guard the area. It's sealed off, of course.' They descended a flight of stairs and de Bok turned left.

'This tunnel goes under Broad Street, you know,' Kris said to Jessima, and de Bok gave a stifled laugh. 'Yes and no,' he said. 'It does, but we are going the other way, towards the Radcliffe Camera. A small area of the book stack is there, and that's where we found the body. I say 'we': I mean our Library Engineer found it when he was doing his rounds. There is one part of the tunnel that goes to the New Library. It houses the conveyor that takes the books to the reading rooms, but it doesn't extend to this side. Staff working this side have to push trolleys.'

De Bok slowed up. 'We're here,' he said. Enormous bookshelves, like free-standing walls, confronted them, each with a large wheel-lock on the front end.

'It's like something out of a submarine!' exclaimed Jessima.

'Designed by Gladstone himself: quite amazing, still in use today - makes maximum use of space, you see.'

'More to the point,' Kris heard himself say, 'we have one

dead body here today. May I see it, please?'

'Of course.' De Bok motioned to the central area where two bookcases now stood well apart, having been wound open by the Library Engineer who had spotted the body squashed between them. The corpse now lay spread across the floor where it had fallen.

'Surely these bookcases are a huge safety risk?' asked Kris.

'Well, no, not really. They are weighted so that any normal person could push them apart, in the unlikely event that one of them should move.'

'But they did,' said Kris.

'So it seems,' said de Bok, somewhat abashed. 'A woman's strength - maybe she was feeling faint, or something... ' His voice trailed off. Jessima gave a cross between a sniff and a grunt.

'I assume you have women staff working down here?' she asked.

'Oh, yes, certainly. About as many women as men, actually.'

'Hum,' said Jessima, which seemed to mean, it couldn't have been an accident, I rest my case.

Kris looked down at the body of Dr Ishbail MacDonald, Keeper of Scientific Books. Mid-fifties, smartly dressed and clearly very dead.

'A highly respected member of staff: only the second woman ever to have been a Keeper; Head of Department, that is,' de Bok explained. 'This is a tragedy. I don't understand it. What happens next, Inspector?'

'Dr Levitt, our pathologist, will be here soon with the rest of the team. She'll examine the body in situ, then it will be taken to the police mortuary,' Kris explained. 'Now, can you tell me a bit more about Dr MacDonald?'

Kris and Jessima returned to the Station with knowledge that only deepened the mystery. As Keeper of Scientific Books, Dr MacDonald was Head of the Radcliffe Science Library, and while she had the right, as a Keeper, to go anywhere within the Bodleian group of libraries, there was no earthly reason why she should visit that particular book stack at the main site so early in the morning. She could, of course, have been there all night, but Dr Levitt's report, when it arrived later in the week, confirmed that this had not been the case. The victim had breakfasted. Stomach contents revealed toast, coffee and a not inconsiderable dose of barbiturates.

Kris assumed they would have some time in which to put together a theory, given the pace at which things moved at the Bodleian Library - or rather, didn't move. However, he was much mistaken.

The Keeper of Printed Books was a dapper little man, somewhat deaf, but like his fellow Keepers an expert in his own field. Hardly recovered from the funeral of his erstwhile colleague, Dr Powell was making his weekly visit to the editorial team who produced the Bodleian Staff Newsletter. They occupied a room on the third floor of the Clarendon Building, in which there are many offices, but no reading rooms. On the ground, first and second floors are what look like cannon-balls left over from the Civil War. It is anyone's guess whether they really are cannon-balls: in any case they make excellent door-stops.

Business completed, Dr Powell descended the stairs. Somewhere above, a door swung shut. Then, suddenly, a sound, gathering momentum, stone on stone. By the time it registered with him and he swung round, one of the cannon-balls was bowling between his feet and Dr Powell went crashing over, tumbling down and down to the ground floor where he might have survived with bruises and a broken bone or two, but for the fact that his head struck the corner of a wrought iron door-scraper, bizarrely kept indoors against theft.

A gloved hand rested on the banister as the person it belonged to stepped round the prone Dr Powell and continued down to the basement, to be concealed in the disused prison cell which still remains next to the cleaner's cubby-hole. Various office doors opened as staff started to investigate the crashing sounds.

After a suitable length of time, long after the ambulance

had come and gone, the owner of the gloved hand left by the back door, crossed the tiny basement garden and went out through the small iron gate into Catte Street.

The Keeper of Printed Books departed this life at 8.25 that evening in the John Radcliffe Hospital: and, at the same time, Kris Lipinski started a massive headache. The Clarendon Building did not lend itself to forensic testing: none of the staff, tucked away in their individual offices on different floors, had witnessed the actual incident, only the aftermath; and, on top of that, quite a few of them believed the basement was haunted anyway. 'To lose one Keeper may be considered unfortunate, but to lose two is downright carelessness,' Dr Levitt misquoted. This did not help Kris's headache.

At the end of the same week came an agitated phone call from the Secretary of the Library. 'You'll never believe this,' Dr de Bok said, 'but we've got another death on our hands. She's lying at the bottom of the Radcliffe Camera stairs - she's definitely dead.'

Kris said that, of course, they would be there as quickly as possible. He replaced the phone, grabbed his jacket and looked for Jessima. 'This is truly weird,' he told her as they headed to his car. 'My father used to say something about believing six impossible things before breakfast. This case is beginning to feel like that!'

'Is that a quaint old Polish saying?' asked Jessima.

'No, a quaint old English one, so far as I know. Something my father picked up after the War. Don't even start me on Polish sayings.'

They looked down at the body of the Keeper of Western Manuscripts. Mrs Anne Shackleton lay sprawled across the marble at the foot of a magnificent curved staircase. Kris gazed upward. No rail or banister on the wide side of the curved stone, nothing she could grab at.

'She's wearing a full-length dress and a jacket,' said Jessima, 'and earrings. It's almost like an Edwardian costume.'

'So?' queried Kris.

'I mean she's dressed more for a party than for work.'

'Hum,' Kris acknowledged. 'People wear anything and everything in Oxford as far as I can see.'

The Porter remembered Mrs Shackleton arriving in her role as Duty Officer for her first check of the day. 'All the Keepers take their turns being on call,' he explained, 'plus one or two of the other most senior staff. That's who we would contact if anything unusual cropped up.'

The main doors opened and de Bok put his head round cautiously. He didn't actually enter. 'Excuse me, sorry, I was just wondering when you will be able to move the, eh, you know... The thing is, we've stopped readers coming in, but eventually someone up in the reading rooms is going to want to come out.'

'Actually, it's a miracle no one's come downstairs yet to use the toilets,' the porter said, interrupting. 'They're on the lower level,' he added to Kris and Jessima.

'So you could be working away up there and have to come all the way down to the basement to find a loo?' Jessima asked.

'They're lucky they've got electricity. And they only got that in the 1930s. It's a Grade I listed building, you know!' He turned to address Dr de Bok. 'I think we ought to get some screens, don't you?' De Bok scuttled away to see what there might be in the sick room.

'You're remarkably calm,' Kris said to the porter.

'Used to be an undertaker,' was the reply. 'This is a semi-retirement job for me, less heavy, if you follow. Most of the time, that is.'

'How extraordinary,' said Jessima, 'from undertaker to library porter.'

'Not really - there's another ex-undertaker over the road at Trinity College - Head Porter he is. A lot of the lads used to be up at Cowley with the motor works. They retire, want a bit of part-time work to pay for holidays and such like, so they end up at places like this.'

'Ah,' said Kris, 'makes sense.' The screens arrived, by the looks of them purchased probably about the same time the electricity was installed. Kris and de Bok were struggling to open them when two students emerged from a reading room and looked down the stairwell; that was when the screaming started.

'She died of a broken neck, according to your report,' said Kris to Miriam Levitt.

'Yes, absolutely. But what made her fall? It has to be said she was clearly anorexic. And I suspect, very clever but very eccentric.'

'Yes, look at how she was dressed, for a start,' interrupted Jessima. 'The staff said she dressed like that all the time.'

'True. There were barbiturates in her stomach contents that would have made her unsteady, but what finally did for her was a dropped hem on her long skirt. She caught one of her heels in it - they were three inch ones - lost her balance and fell. There was thread and material round her left heel, and a hole in the dress material.'

'So her death was an accident in the end,' said Kris, 'but the drugs in her system - that's a bit of a coincidence, isn't it?'

'Might be, might not,' replied Miriam Levitt. 'She may have been taking pain-killers habitually; she wasn't a healthy woman.'

Kris sighed. Another loose end. His Chief would not be pleased. 'Well, we can check with her GP,' he said.

Dr Adrian Hastings, Keeper of Oriental Books, was the only remaining Keeper when the date of a dinner at his old college, marking his forty years of service to the Bodleian Library, came round. The deaths didn't worry him unduly. His thoughts were centred on his speech and what his colleagues would make of it. It was a pity, of course, that so many of them would miss it. However, some senior members of staff remained, plus many important university figures and other guests from the world of Oriental Studies.

His speech went down well, and the highlight of the evening was a complete surprise. Dr Hastings was presented with an oriental dagger, a perfect replica of a rare and ancient artefact that resided in the Ashmolean Museum. He was delighted with it and, walking back to the Bodleian where his car was parked in its exclusive Keeper's slot, was heard to mention that he would bring it in again the next day to show everyone at work.

He did not arrive home. Mrs Hastings reported him missing the next morning, and his car was found to be still at the Library.

Kris and Jessima drove to the Bodleian in grim silence until Jessima spoke. 'Are you thinking what I'm thinking?' she said. 'That this will be the last murder?'

'Because it's the fourth and there are four keepers?' replied Kris, 'Four deaths and three murders, technically speaking, but I'm sure Mrs Shackleton was destined to be a victim. Still, we won't know until we catch the killer.' As he got out of the car he instructed Jessima to interview the porters. 'And find out if there's anything on the CCTV.'

'Doubt it,' Jessima said. 'Hasn't been working for weeks, one of the porters told me yesterday.'

Kris decided to 'walk the course', revisiting the scenes of the murders. He was accompanied by the Library Engineer, Mr Allan, with his set of master keys. It was Mr Allan who spotted, as they walked across the Old Schools Quadrangle, that a particular paving stone did not look right. One corner was up and the opposite corner was chipped. 'Someone's lifted that,' he said. 'Moved it single-handed and all.'

'Can that be done?' Kris asked.

'It's made to be movable. It's the way to the underground water tanks,' Mr Allan explained as he and Kris lifted the stone between them. 'They were put in during the War in case Oxford was bombed - been there ever since.' Neither of them was really surprised to see Dr Hastings staring up at the sky from his watery coffin, the hilt of the dagger like some gruesome Excalibur in his chest.

Kris headed towards the Secretary's office to make the necessary telephone calls. Dr de Bok was not there, and he was received by the PA, Maryla Dakowska.

After a brief chat about their shared Polish heritage, Kris made his phone calls, then got down to business. Yes, Dr de Bok was usually early, and it wasn't like him not to say if he was going to be late. Maryla offered to ring his home number and see what was happening. Mrs de Bok confirmed that her husband had only just left for work, much later than usual and, yes, she would say he was agitated. She couldn't talk long; she had to go and attend to her elderly mother - who, Maryla explained to Kris, lived with the de Boks, and was in very poor health, with increasingly bad pain that the strongest opiates did not seem to control.

In the next half hour Kris learned more from Maryla about how the Library ran than he had from anyone else. Tradition had it that Bodley's Librarian should always be selected from among the Keepers. Less traditionally, it seemed that Dr de Bok despised the lot of them. 'He thinks they couldn't organise a chimps' tea party,' Maryla told Kris. 'He has no respect for their scholarship, and believes the Library could be run far more efficiently by a good administrator such as himself.'

There were two ways in to the Secretary's Office: the main one, through Maryla's office, and a smaller side door leading to a lobby, where there was another door to a meeting room. Kris looked up to see Jessima entering by the main door, flourishing a CCTV tape. 'I was wrong! The camera was working - you'll never guess, but it's proof - ' She stopped short and her eyes widened, looking behind Kris to the side door. He turned quickly: framed in the doorway, as if frozen, stood Dr de Bok.

De Bok turned on his heels and ran. Quick as they were to react, the few seconds' lag as they dodged the office furniture meant that they emerged into the quadrangle uncertain of where he had gone. Then a door banged in the arch where the Great Gate opens under the Tower of the Five Orders. 'He's gone up the tower,' Maryla gasped. 'That little wooden door - he's used his master keys.'

'Anyone else up there?' asked Kris.

'A few, it's where the University Archives are.'

'Can we ring an office in there?'

'Of course,' said Maryla, 'come on.' She and Kris ran back to her office. Jessima, walking backwards, gazed up at the Tower with its magnificent columns as if she was willing it to tell her what it knew. She didn't have to wait long. A figure appeared on a small balcony near the top: de Bok.

Jessima didn't know afterwards whether she screamed or shouted. She was trying to say, No, stop, wait: but it was too late. Kris emerged from the Schola Metaphysicae door just in time to see de Bok jump. No one, certainly not the small crowd that had gathered, wanted to look at what lay at their feet.

'It just shows what can happen when an intelligent mind goes horribly wrong,' Miriam Levitt observed. 'Obviously de Bok had become totally obsessed with the idea that he would be elected Bodley's Librarian if only the Keepers were out of the way.'

'Yes,' agreed Kris. 'And he had access to his mother-in-law's drugs, knew everyone's movements, every inch of the buildings. Above all, he had master keys. If it hadn't been for the CCTV working, he might just have got away with it. Whatever people's suspicions, there'd have been no proof.'

'I wonder what will happen to the Library now,' said Jessima.

'I asked Maryla that,' replied Kris. 'She says they'll advertise the post properly and hold interviews. Probably a total outsider will be appointed. Maybe someone from one of the other great libraries - even someone from abroad. She said it will be a fresh start and possibly the best thing all round.'

'We'll have to go back and see,' said Jessima. 'Perhaps it would be worth getting readers' tickets after all.'

RURAL BLISS

ANGELA CECIL-REID

Some twenty miles north-west of Oxford stands the market town of Chipping Norton, gateway to the rolling Cotswold Hills with their open fields and lattice of stone walls. Beneath the hills, quiet villages of golden limestone nestle in wooded valleys.

Apple Blossom Cottage was situated in one such village. It had been described by the estate agents as "a Cotswold gem set in a garden of picturebook perfection, along with an extensive and mature apple orchard." The brochure had continued, "this is your once-in-a-lifetime opportunity to buy this piece of rural bliss - do not miss out."

Margaret and Robert Sparrow had indeed decided not to miss out, and had given up the pavements and tarmac of Birmingham to buy their "piece of rural bliss".

The leaves in the orchard were turning scarlet when Margaret went down one morning to collect apples to make a pie for Robert's supper. She was not immediately alarmed when an ageing Land Rover, towing a small battered trailer, pulled up in front of the orchard gate. She only realised what was being delivered when a squat red-faced farmer dropped the tailgate and released five large, white and extraordinarily woolly sheep, with Rastafarian fringes, into the orchard.

'My God! What are these?' she heard herself asking.

The farmer stared at her, raised a grubby hand and scratched thoughtfully at his scalp. At last he said, 'Why, they be sheep, Mrs Sparrow.'

'I can see that! But what are they doing here?'

He looked at her with bright eyes. 'They might ask you that, Mrs Sparrow. They be Cotswold sheep and they bin on these hills since Roman times. There were thousands of 'em. Now they be a *rare breed*.' His final words were loaded with dark emphasis.

'But why are they in my orchard?' demanded Margaret.

'Well, I meets Mr. Sparrow last week, and he said you would be looking for summat to cut the grass. Says I, what you needs is a few sheep. No petrol needed, no time sitting going round in circles. Just leave 'em to it. So says he, that sounds like a good idea, Mr Jones. Then I says I'll drop 'em off. And here they be.'

'But Robert told me we're getting a ride-on tractor mower. We don't need to borrow any sheep.'

'Borrow? These be bought and paid for, and they be registered, with names.' With that he shut the back of the trailer, handed her five certificates, climbed into his Land Rover and rattled off, leaving Margaret to close the gate behind him. She glanced at the certificates. The sheep did indeed have names - India, Isabel, Ida, Irma and Irene. She looked at the five sheep. Which was which? They all looked identical to her. Anyway, why should she care? They would all be gone tomorrow.

She hurried back down the path towards the house, her stilettos sinking into the soft earth, brambles tearing at her silk skirt. Ridiculous, she thought. They knew nothing about sheep. In fact they knew nothing about any animals. She closed the door firmly behind her. There had been some dreadful mistake. Robert would sort it out the moment he returned.

As Margaret waited for him that evening, she wondered if their rural dream was quite as perfect as it had initially seemed. They had been so pleased when Robert had been offered relocation to the Oxford branch of Be Prepared Insurance plc. The office was at the heart of the city, in the shadow of Queen's College in the High Street, and they would live at Apple Blossom Cottage, a mere thirty minutes' commute away.

Robert arrived home exhausted: the new job involved longer hours than he had expected. He had no interest in the sheep beyond, 'So they've come. Good.'

When Margaret complained at some length that she had neither the time, nor desire, to look after sheep, he sighed. 'Sheep don't need looking after. They'll just eat the grass that I won't have the time to mow.'

And he looked so tired that she changed the subject. 'I've made your favourite for dinner. Shepherd's pie.'

The following morning she walked down to the orchard. The sheep were contentedly munching their way through the ragged carpet of autumn grass. She realised that they looked just right; as if they had lived in the orchard always.

The sheep lifted their heads when she opened the gate, and trotted over to her, so that she was surrounded by a wave of pushing noses. Margaret noticed that each sheep was wearing a numbered tag. She pulled the certificates out of her pocket and saw that those had not just a name but a number too. So that's how she could work out which sheep was which, if she wanted to: but she didn't.

The sheep began to bleat plaintively. They were after something, but what? She needed advice and rang Mr Jones. He was happy to help. 'I'll send young Joe round, he knows them sheep like the back of his hand.'

Young Joe duly arrived. He was in his forties, taller than his father, but with the same solid build. 'You want to know about these here sheep. I suppose you don't have 'em where you come from.'

'No,' Margaret agreed.

Joe had brought a large bucket with him, and shook it vigorously. The sheep trotted briskly towards him. ''Tis nuts they want. Rattle a bucket and they'll follow you anywhere. He looked at her. 'Littl'uns love sheep. You got any?'

Margaret shook her head and sighed. That pain belonged to a distant world of hospitals, tests and monthly disappointment. 'No,' she said softly, 'no children.'

Joe must have heard the sadness in her voice for he gave her a small, lop-sided smile before changing the subject. 'I think it'll fair pour it down tonight.'

Over the next few months Joe visited frequently. He helped her shear the ewes, worm them, and vaccinate them against unpronounceable diseases. One day he arrived with a book entitled *Lambing for Beginners*.

'Oh, I won't need this,' said Margaret.

Joe stared at her with copper-brown eyes. 'I think you will. Look at the size of them ewes. They be due about the beginning of April.'

Margaret had been congratulating herself that very morning on how well her flock were doing on the early spring grass. She looked at their swelling bellies afresh. Of course they were pregnant: they looked like overfilled rugby balls bursting at their laces.

Now each morning when she woke she hurried to the window and watched the white shapes grazing peacefully amongst the apple trees. Whatever the weather, she leaned out of her window and called, 'Good morning, girls.'

For a while Robert said nothing, but one Monday morning he snapped. 'For God's sake, Margaret, do you ever think about anything except those bloody sheep? The house is a tip, and you look a complete mess.' He picked up his briefcase and a small black hold-all. 'I'll be away till Wednesday. The Paris office has a problem. You can get things sorted while I'm gone.' The front door slammed shut.

It was true, thought Margaret, looking round the bedroom at the piles of clothes scattered over the floor, that her life and her house were almost unrecognisable. She pulled on a pair of mud-spattered jeans and a baggy jumper, and hurried downstairs.

Life is so good, she thought, as she sat in the pale spring sunshine some weeks later, painting the girls as they grazed nearby. As her brush feathered each stroke and the ewes came to life on the page, she felt utterly content.

When the afternoon turned to dusk, she gradually became aware of some restlessness in the flock. She looked up from her work and saw Ida alone by the hedge, pawing at the ground. Margaret remembered that this was one sign of lambing. She sat on the gate and waited. Robert would have to manage his own Heat and Serve Fisherman's Pie.

Dusk turned to moonlit night before Ida lay down and, with her head arching backwards, began to strain. Margaret watched, transfixed. Eventually a glistening bundle slithered out into the moonlight. Ida struggled to her feet and began licking her lamb. Unbelievably soon the tiny thing lifted its head and rose unsteadily to its feet like a badly-handled puppet. Just then a second bundle dropped to the ground. Margaret smiled as she made her way back to the house.

'We've got twins,' she told the snoring Robert.

He grunted, then peered at her through half-closed eyes and muttered, 'More bloody sheep.'

It was three weeks later, and all the ewes but Isabel had lambed. Margaret slept little. Every four hours she would climb out of bed to check the sheep.

Then, one morning in the cold greyness just before dawn, Margaret found Isabel lying in the shed, exhausted, and with no lamb in sight. She rang Joe and he arrived fifteen minutes later. 'There, there, girl, I'll soon have you sorted,' he soothed, and plunged his arm inside the sheep.

He looked up at Margaret. 'She's got three, all jumbled up in here.' A few minutes later, after three firm pulls, he laid three steaming packages on the grass. Two of them at once began to twitch and wriggle, but the smallest lay motionless.

'Oh no! It's dead,' Margaret whispered.

'Don't stand there gawping,' Joe commanded, 'Clean out its mouth and nose, then rub it with straw. And if that don't work, then you pick it up by its back legs and spin it.'

Margaret picked up a handful of straw and began rubbing frantically at the lamb; but it lay as still as death. There was no time to lose. She took hold of its legs and swung it wildly round before depositing it back on the straw. It lay there unmoving for an endless second, but all of a sudden it sneezed and twitched. Isabel began licking it dry.

Joe sat back on his haunches and studied the group. 'That there ewe'll not manage three on her own. You'll have to help by bottling the littl'un.'

Margaret looked at the tiny white lamb she had resuscitated, with its ridiculously long legs and black button nose, and fell in love. 'Jenny,' she whispered, 'I'll call her Jenny.'

'For Heaven's sake, why Jenny?' said her exasperated husband later.

'I like the name,' said Margaret, remembering the

daughter she had never had.

Every four hours she would make up a bottle of Lamb Save: as she held it for the frantically sucking lamb, she felt complete in a way she never had before.

The summer passed and the lambs seemed to grow bigger each day. Robert was often abroad now, sometimes in Amsterdam or even Prague. He could be away for weeks at a time. Margaret grew used to his absence.

One night in early autumn when Robert arrived home, he found no dinner at all waiting for him. Indeed Margaret looked at him as if she was not quite sure who he was.

'Aren't those bloody lambs ready to go yet?'

'Go? Where?' Margaret stared at him, her mouth open.

'To Carvers. The abattoir, of course.'

Margaret looked at him as if he had said that the world would end in five minutes. 'My lambs will never end up on a plate,' she said icily. Then with as much dignity as she could muster she stalked off down the path to the orchard.

The word "abattoir" was not mentioned again, and in all other ways their lives continued as usual, until a letter arrived inviting Margaret to a school reunion.

'You really must go,' said Robert. 'It'll be good for you to catch up with people you haven't seen for thirty years.' He had not been this encouraging about anything for so long, and his enthusiasm took Margaret by surprise. She would ask him to keep an eye on the girls, just for the day.

On Tuesday, two weeks later, Margaret drove up to Birmingham and had a most pleasurable time catching up with her old classmates. As she drove back, she reflected that, much as she adored her girls, it was refreshing to have a break from them occasionally.

It was dark when she arrived home and she was exhausted. She went straight to bed. Robert was already snoring contentedly. Yet, as she dropped off to sleep, she had a nagging feeling that something was wrong...

The sound of plaintive bleating woke her. Robert was still asleep, and the cold bleak light of dawn was only just breaking as she pulled on her clothes and hurried outside.

When she arrived at the orchard gate, she saw instantly

that the lambs were not there. Fighting to control her rising panic she checked the fences, but there were no gaps. She searched for tyre marks. It didn't take long for her to spot the tracks that led away from the gate. She tore up the path to the cottage and, flinging open the bedroom door, shouted, 'Robert, wake up. My babies have been stolen. Ring the police.'

Robert rolled over and looked blearily up at her. 'Get a grip, woman. Mr Jones took them to Carvers yesterday. You weren't going to organise it, so I did.'

Margaret stared open-mouthed at her husband, shock distorting her lips into a ghastly grin. 'You sent Jenny to the abattoir?'

And he grinned back at her. 'Of course. And if you're interested, I've resigned. Too much travelling. We're moving back to Birmingham. Then the rest of the sheep can go to Carvers too.' He shut his eyes, but his lips were still smiling.

Margaret stared down at him. Rage and grief clutched at her throat, strangling her. She hated him then more than she had hated anyone in her entire life.

In late October Margaret invited several of her old classmates to lunch. It was an unusually warm day and they ate on the patio, which gave them an excellent view of the orchard where the girls were grazing peacefully. She could see Joe perched on the roof of the old apple store. It was kind of him to mend it for her. He was always so helpful, and really he was quite attractive in an earthy sort of way.

'Joe's a bit of all right!' said Melissa glancing sideways at Margaret. 'What's Robert up to at the moment?'

Margaret gave a small smile. 'Oh, I'm afraid he's away on business. Abroad. Prague actually. Won't be back for ages. Maybe months.'

'It must be so lonely for you,' said Anna, sympathising.

Margaret shrugged. 'Not really. I have Joe to help out, and of course my girls keep me busy.' She took the lid off the casserole in front of her, and the air was filled with an unusually rich spiciness mingled with hints of apricot and honey. Margaret smiled: it was the first meal she had cooked in ages, and it seemed worth all the effort. She began ladling the meat onto plates and passing them round. 'Do help yourselves to salad,' she told her guests.

'This casserole is quite superb. The meat is so wonderfully tender. Aren't you having any?' asked Sarah.

'Oh, no… thank you. I'll just stick with the salad. But I'm delighted you're enjoying it. I did make sure the meat was well hung,' Margaret assured her.

It was only then that she noticed the row of empty glasses lining the table. 'My goodness. The wine. I'll find the corkscrew.'

In the kitchen, Margaret searched the drawers. She was sure Robert had had it last. Where would he have left it? She pulled open the drawer by the sink where all the essentials were kept, everything from matches to insurance certificates. She paused. Robert won't be needing those, she thought, and picked up a small folder, along with a box of matches and the missing corkscrew.

She carried everything into the sitting room. It was cool, even on such a lovely day as this. A fire would be just the thing to take away the chill. She crossed to the fireplace and struck a match.

It was only a matter of seconds before the wood began to spark and glow. She methodically emptied the contents of the folder onto the fire. The papers burst into flames almost immediately. But the passport took longer. Margaret watched the edges smoulder, and then suddenly the whole booklet curled and blackened. Dust to dust, she thought, ashes to ashes. Then she picked up the corkscrew again and went outside.

'Now, who would like some wine?' she asked cheerfully.

THE FESTIVAL OF INTERNATIONAL ART AND SCHOLARLY CULTURE OXFORD

JANE GORDON-CUMMING

' ...So we need to structure a scheme to maximise the potential of this unique opportunity.'

It was a warm afternoon. Oxford hummed gently through the open window, a soothing sound like a distantly busy bee. A pair of pigeons was courting on the roof opposite, strutting round with little respect for the ancient stonework, their cooing seductively hypnotic. The Arts Committee had had a good lunch, courtesy of the college whose room they were using, and now it felt dangerously like nap time. They made an effort to pull themselves together and attend to what the new Director was saying.

'With Britain the focus of the world's eyes in this Olympic year, we must make sure a great city like ours doesn't get left on the periphery of international vision.'

'Oh yes, that would be a terrible pity.' How beautiful the Director's own eyes were! - that deep blue, and the way they crinkled at the corners.

'I'm so glad you agree with me, Barbara.' He turned them on the Secretary, making her feel warm and valued and special.

Grace, who had begun to sketch the courting pigeons, made them into peacocks, with large eyes on their tails.

'Oxford is a mere stone's throw from the Olympic village,' the Director went on, 'when you're talking about visitors from China and the States.' One could tell, from the familiar way he spoke, that he had actually been to America. 'We need to find a way of putting it on the map.'

'I rather thought Oxford was on the map already!' Their Academic Representative, a minor English don, smiled archly round at the rest of them. 'The tourists down there in the High certainly seem to think so.'

'On the map metaphorically speaking, I mean.' The Director smiled back at him in a kindly way, leaving everyone with the impression that Max had been stupid, rather than witty. 'We may not be able to provide Triple Jumping and Badminton, but I believe we can offer our own contribution, celebrating what Oxford does best - Culture.'

'What kind of event did you have in mind, Ran?' His name was Ranulph, but he'd told them to call him Ran. Barbara waited, pen in hand, notebook at the ready.

'A grand Festival of all the Arts. And I'm hoping that you're going to help me make it one of the most attractive events on the programme.'

The Committee murmured excitedly. It was some time since they'd actually been asked to do anything.

'Oh cool!' said the pretty student who represented Young People. 'You mean, like people's paintings and stuff?'

Grace, the only artist on the Arts Committee, glanced up.

'I was imagining something a little more adventurous, Sophie,' Ran said. 'Figurative art is so last century, don't you think? I'm seeing installations, performance pieces, experiment and innovation... ' Grace returned her attention to her drawing.

'An opportunity for talented people who wouldn't normally get the chance to present their work,' nodded Max. Barbara did hope he wasn't going to offer to read his poetry.

'I'm not sure I like the word talent,' Ran objected. 'Connotations of elitism, don't you think? We want to include the whole community, not just those of us who happen to be artistically gifted - make the Little Guy feel he has a role to play.' Their hearts warmed, as Ran's eyes took on the caring expression of a man prepared to champion the Little Guy. 'But time is short, so we need to get this balloon in the air quickly. Come at me with ideas, people!'

There was the inevitable silence. Everyone was keen to contribute, but their minds had gone suddenly blank.

'Street Art,' Amita, their legal expert, suggested at last.

'You know - like Banksy? There are an awful lot of bare walls in Oxford.'

'Oh yes,' said Barbara eagerly, 'Longwall, and the backs of the colleges in Turl Street. They could do with cheering up.'

'Wouldn't it be rather a shame to daub paint on those lovely old buildings?'

But nobody took any notice of Grace.

'I've got a friend who does fab sculptures,' put in Sophie. 'They're made out of plants and stuff, so they're, like, really green as well.'

'Excellent.' Ran beamed at her. 'We should aim to give this a minimal carbon foot-print.'

'In that case,' said Max, 'I hope you're going to include the spoken word... '

'We must be sure to get the children involved,' said Barbara quickly. 'My primary class had a wonderful time decorating the streets for our village fête last year. And the differently abled, and people who are - er - ,' she struggled to find the right phrase, 'challenged about their sexuality. And ethnic minorities, of course.' She smiled across at Amita.

'Any kid painting the streets of Oxford is likely to be mown down by a bus,' Max observed.

The Committee tutted, either at this appalling thought, or the somewhat gleeful tone with which he expressed it.

'Naturally whatever space we use will need to be traffic free,' said Ran. 'We'll close off Broad Street. I'm sure places like Blackwell's and the Bodleian won't object for such a major cultural event.'

'Will one road be enough, do you think?' Sophie looked worried. 'My friend's sculptures are kind of - like - big.'

Everyone brightened up at the thought of having a few Angels of the North around, especially Max, whose college was rather jealous of Exeter's Antony Gormley.

'We can always extend round the corner into St. Giles,' he suggested. 'They use it for the Fair, after all.'

'Oh yeah, cool. Though we might need to move that spiky thing out of the way. You know,' Sophie explained when the others looked blank, 'Martha's Memorial. Who was Martha, anyway?'

'We'll need permission from the Council to close the roads,' Amita warned them, 'and Public Liability insurance.'

'Right.' Ran glanced at his watch. 'Well, we've some fantastic ideas here. Let's get them actioned... Barbara, I want you to find me a graffiti artist who will be the Oxford Banksy. Will you do that for me?'

She'd do anything for Ran when he looked at her like that, even if she'd never heard of Banksy.

'Max, you're our academic bod. I'll put you in charge of the school kids.'

'What? Oh, I don't know. I'm not really... '

'Oh, you'll simply love working with children!' Barbara assured him somewhat enviously. 'It's such a privilege to watch the little ones giving rein to their creativity. You don't need much in the way of materials, just some big brushes, and you can get that special stuff that washes off... '

'I am capable of buying paint, thank you, Barbara.'

'The trouble with involving children in art,' Grace observed, 'is that they can't do it. They simply make a mess.'

But everyone ignored this heresy.

'Amita, you can be our Equal Opportunities Officer,' said Ran. 'Make sure we've got plenty of artists who are black, or women, or have something else wrong with them. ...Sophie, you're going to be our Location Manager.'

'Oh cool!' She sat up proudly.

'You'll need to liaise with the colleges and shops in Broad Street. Explain how important it is, and they might let us use some of their premises for exhibition space... Um, Grace.' He glanced at his notes. 'You can sort out any permits and insurance we need.'

Grace wrote "permit" and "insurance" on the corner of her drawing.

'So has everyone got a job now?' Everyone had, except Ran.

'The Oxford Festival of Art and Culture,' sighed Barbara. 'Doesn't it sound lovely?'

'International Art and Culture,' Ran corrected. 'Don't forget this is to attract our foreign visitors - and rather more "now" for "Oxford" to go at the end, don't you think?'

'Speaking as an academic,' said Max, 'I do feel a reference to our scholarly heritage should go in somewhere.'

Barbara altered her notes and read them out. 'Here we are, then: the Festival of International Art and Scholarly Culture Oxford.'

Everyone murmured happily at this satisfactory amalgam of their individual concerns. Only Grace stared at what she had written down. She had the feeling that something wasn't quite right about it.

Jerrold was at a bit of a loose end. He usually hung about in a gang with his mates at this time of the evening, but none of his mates were around, and it's hard to look cool in a gang of one. The wall beside him was a mess of tags and cartoons. Someone had left a can of paint beside it, and Jerrold picked it up, wondering whether to try his hand at adding OUFC, or go home for his tea.

'Hey!'

Shit, that woman had clocked him! Jerrold stopped in the act of shaking the can and tried to hide it behind his back. She reminded him of his primary school teacher.

'Oh hello, Jerrold.' It was his primary school teacher! Double shit. 'Were you about to spray paint on that wall?'

'No, Miss,' he responded automatically.

But she wasn't listening. 'Come along with me, dear, - and bring that with you.'

Jerrold followed her with a resigned sigh. Was she going to haul him off to the Police Station - or worse, back home to have a word with his mum?

'You want us to move out *all* our books?' The lady at the Bodleian was a little startled.

'Yes, I'm really sorry, but it's - like - for this really important cultural festival thing,' Sophie explained apologetically.

'Oh well.' The lady shrugged at the vagaries of the Powers That Be. 'I suppose they can go to Swindon with the rest of our stock.'

The man at Blackwell's took rather more persuading. 'But this is a bookshop! We can't just get rid of all our books.'

'Oh, but you've simply *got* to,' Sophie pleaded. 'Otherwise there won't be enough room for our exhibitions and stuff. It would be absolutely *dire*.'

He weakened at the sight of an anxious tear hovering on those long eyelashes. 'But how are we supposed to make a living? You really can't expect us to close the shop at the height of the tourist season.'

'Oh no, we're not asking you to close it!' Sophie hastened to reassure him on that point. 'People will still be able to come into the shop - it's just that there won't be all these books in the way.'

Grace found her sketch when she was searching her bag for a shopping list. Worth keeping? No, a mere doodle. Nothing she couldn't recreate from her imagination if required. She was about to scrunch it up, when she noticed something written on the corner. Aha! Lucky she'd had the sense to make those notes.

It was with a feeling of great satisfaction that she picked up the phone and renewed first her parking permit and then her house insurance. Who said that she tended to be forgetful?

Max had never been into a DIY store. Responsibility for repairs or decoration in Max's life had rested with his college or his landlady, and before that with his public school. Even his parents had always got a Little Man in. But now Max was required to buy paint, and he wouldn't want anyone to think he was so out of touch that he didn't know where to obtain it. Feeling like Livingstone seeking the source of the Nile, he ventured up the Botley Road.

This must be the right place. The store proclaimed that it supplied everything a builder or decorator might want, and there was even a picture of a ladder and a pot of paint for those who couldn't read. Inside was an Aladdin's cave, rows and rows of tins in every possible hue. Max filled a trolley with a selection of bright primary colours, added a pack of brushes, and tagged on to the queue of builders and do-it-yourselfers at the check-out, feeling a trifle smug at how easy it was to join their club.

'Nice bright colours these,' said the lady as she scanned in the tins. 'Just the thing for doing up a playroom.'

She looked a question Max didn't bother to answer, but he suddenly remembered something Barbara had mentioned.

'I suppose this stuff is washable?'

'Oh yes, completely,' the woman assured him. 'Wipe it with a damp cloth and you'll find it comes up clean as anything. Perfect for kiddies.'

Max left the store with the satisfaction of knowing he'd got exactly the right thing.

'Couldn't you move it back just a teensy little bit?' Sophie pleaded. 'You know, like you do for St. Giles' Fair?'

'I'm not sure we actually move the College for the Fair,' said the young lady on the phone, doubtfully. She was the Acting Deputy Assistant Bursar's Deputy Assistant, standing in on a temporary basis while the Acting Deputy Assistant Bursar's Deputy was away on maternity leave, and she wasn't completely *au fait* with College procedure.

'You wouldn't need to move the whole thing,' Sophie explained to her, 'just that bit sticking out at the front. It so - like - completely blocks the road.'

'Yes, it does rather,' the ADABDA had to admit. Oh dear, she wished they hadn't left her in sole charge! Would she be authorised to demolish extraneous parts of the college?

But Ran had entrusted Sophie with the job of making sure the Festival had enough space, and she was determined not to let him down. She sensed the girl wavering, and pressed home.

'You could always put something similar back afterwards, and pretend it was the same building all the time, like they did with the Ashmolean.'

'Oh yes, we could call it "refurbishment". And there's

that big crane in the back garden, waiting for them to start work on the new accommodation block. They're always telling us to economise on resources... '

'So the cool thing is, you'd actually be saving the college money!'

It was a no-brainer.

'Right, I don't want to keep you long.' Ran had another meeting to go to. 'Just need to check we're all up to speed on the action front and ready to roll.'

'I've found a graffiti artist,' said Barbara proudly. 'He's called Jerrold and he wears a baseball cap. He's black,' she added, to make the point to Amita.

'Yippee,' said their Equal Opportunities Officer. 'I don't suppose he's a lesbian as well? Then I could really tick those little boxes.'

Ran gave her a look which made Barbara quail on her behalf.

With no view from the window - they were in a basement room today - Grace began to sketch her fellow Committee members. Ran's handsome regular features, those perfect eyebrows raised in a little arc of disapproval at Amita's failure to play the game. Barbara's brown puppy eyes round with alarm. Amita's glinting.

'I popped into the DIY store,' said Max, as if he was the sort of man who did that, 'and bought the stuff for the children's project. We're ready to let the little dears loose on the streets with paints and brushes as soon as you fire the gun.'

'I hope there won't be any guns involved, with children around,' said Barbara, who hadn't liked his tone.

'Tamsin's made some absolutely gigantic figures,' reported Sophie. 'And I've cleared the roads and emptied all the buildings, so there'll be loads of room for everything.'

'Excellent,' said Ran. 'I'm in touch with some very promising young artists at the Courtauld. We can give them the Sheldonian. And Tracey's latest installation would look great in the Radcliffe Camera...

'Hang on,' Amita interrupted him. 'I thought this thing

was supposed to be about Oxford culture.'

'Yes,' said Max, 'an opportunity for us to present our own contribution to the Arts.'

' ...Provided we've no artistic talent,' murmured Grace.

The Committee looked at Ran anxiously. What had happened to the Little Guy? Was he not to play his part after all?

'Well yes, of course there'll be a space for local work,' Ran hastened to reassure them. 'I was thinking a nice little display in the Oxfam shop. It's much bigger inside than it looks... but we want to get some decent stuff in as well. International visitors will expect a bit more than the Saturday Art Club!'

The Committee smiled with him, keen to distance themselves from the likes of the Saturday Art Club.

'No, we must give them the best that Oxford can offer, and that means offering them the best,' Ran went on with oracular logic. 'As I said, there's some very exciting work coming out of the London colleges. And I've been talking to Damien's people... '

The Committee exchanged delighted glances; faith was rapidly being restored. The Festival of International Art and Scholarly Culture was going to be a highly prestigious cultural event which would transform the city, and make the people of Oxford proud.

'No one will come,' warned Grace. 'They'll all be watching the Olympics.'

Nobody actually came to the Festival, although they wished it well. Britain was in the running for several medals, and those who weren't able to attend the Olympics in person were watching them on television. When the citizens of Oxford emerged from their curtain-drawn seclusion, they found the whole face of their city had changed.

Jerrold's wobbly 'J', sometimes dripping a little, sometimes smudged a bit, was inscribed on every conceivable blank space: Longwall, the old houses opposite, the new buildings in the science block. Occasionally he'd ventured into a second colour, but mostly it was a vivid, gory red.

The crane driver had leapt at the chance to use the big ball they'd supplied with his crane, and set to work on straightening out that awkward corner of the college with a will. Unfortunately, when the dust died down, they found that he'd also demolished the Chapel, but - as Sophie pointed out - it had been very old and crumbly.

The children had given full rein to their creativity, not only in Broad Street, but St. Giles and a good part of Cornmarket. Bus lanes and cycle paths, yellow lines and parking boxes were now indistinguishable, obscured by a coating of brightly-coloured, hard-wearing, indelible - but completely washable - gloss paint.

And over all hung a pungent, overpowering smell. Sophie's friend's sculptures had fulfilled their promise in every way. Huge (so huge that a group of Japanese businessmen touring the nightspots, who came across their storage place, ran away screaming), and constructed entirely from material discarded on compost heaps, they were now returning to nature even more quickly than predicted. It had been a hot week.

Ran didn't appear at the Debrief Meeting. Rumour had it that he'd lived up to his name and already moved on to a prestigious new job in London.

'Oh well,' sighed Barbara, as she struggled to deal with a massive insurance claim - companies were so naughty about paying up! How could they pretend they'd never received the application? - 'I suppose it would have been selfish to expect to keep a bright star like that for long.' She imagined Ran rocketing up to join the high-flyers across the London skies.

Somebody raised the question of whether to make the Festival an annual event, but the feeling of the Committee was against. Given the lasting impression it had made on the city, one FIASCO, they decided, was quite enough.

IN TIME FOR THE WAKE

HEATHER ROSSER

The tall Nigerian peered intently at the Benin bronzes in their glass display cabinet at the Pitt Rivers Museum.

'They're amazing, aren't they?' said Lisa.

Sam studied the little figures of the king and his retinue a moment longer. Then he turned and smiled at the young woman in her jeans and Fair Trade t-shirt.

'My father works in bronze.'

'How wonderful! Does he make things like this?'

He shook his head. 'We live in a village in the Mandara Mountains. He will sometimes make a mask for a special occasion but more often it is bells or bracelets or drinking vessels.'

Sam's words conjured up a picture in Lisa's mind of an old man sitting in the doorway of a thatched hut, carefully polishing a bronze chalice. The two of them lingered by a display of musical instruments and Sam told her about the tradition in his village of dancing to the drums late into the night whenever there was a full moon.

Lisa blinked when they came out of the museum into the autumn sunshine. The leaves on the trees in University Parks were beginning to turn and by the time they reached Jericho there was a chill in the air.

'We're nearly there,' she said as she noticed Sam put his thumbs through his rucksack for support.

'It is very kind of you and your mother to invite me for the weekend.'

'She's always enjoyed hosting British Council students. Ever since I was a child the house has been full of international students. That's why I wanted to travel.'

'Have you been to Africa?'

Lisa looked wistful. 'I was hoping to go when I'd paid off my student debt. I worked in London for a few years and was in the process of applying for overseas posts when my mother had her accident. So I came back to Oxford.' She hesitated. 'You know she's in a wheelchair?'

'No, they didn't tell me. I hope I won't be too much trouble.' Sam looked concerned.

'You're the first student she's had for five years; she's really looking forward to your visit.'

'And I am looking forward to meeting her.' Sam paused. 'What are those people doing?' he asked as they passed a funeral cortege on the other side of the road, with half a dozen mourners standing on the pavement.

'It's a funeral,' said Lisa and shivered as a sudden wind chased a flurry of dead leaves along the street. She started to hurry on but Sam stood and watched as the coffin was placed in the hearse and the mourners shuffled into their cars.

'Why are there so few people?' he asked incredulously.

Lisa swallowed. 'Maybe the others are waiting at the crematorium.'

'Where my father lives mourners come from all around to give comfort to the bereaved and help the departed soul on its way. We dig the grave ourselves and they are buried within twenty-four hours.'

'But how do you have time to make all the arrangements?''

'The whole family and neighbours stop whatever they are doing and help. But of course not everyone can be notified, especially in these modern days when many people are away from home. That is why a wake is held a year later.'

'A wake?'

'Yes: that is the time when all the family come together and a final feast is held for the departed. Sometimes,' Sam explained earnestly, 'a soul has difficulty in getting to the other side, but when a wake is held the departed know that their time on this earth has ended.'

'It sounds a good way to honour the dead,' Lisa said thoughtfully.

Frost scrunched beneath her tyres as Lisa cycled past the Sheldonian and came to a halt at the Oxfam shop. She locked her bike and paused to admire the colourful Christmas window display before opening up the shop. A woman hurried in for wrapping paper, a calendar and some Fair Trade chocolate. It was early, but Lisa didn't have the heart to turn her away, and she knew that the volunteers would be arriving soon. Managing a charity shop hadn't been in her mind when she graduated with a business degree, but the opportunity had arisen soon after she returned to Oxford to look after her mother, and she found the work both challenging and satisfying.

She glanced appraisingly at the displays of jewellery and exotic gifts, then went upstairs past neat rails of clothes, before hurrying up the final flight and into a room piled high with boxes of donated clothing, books and bric-a-brac waiting to be sorted. She crossed the room and opened the door to her office. While she was waiting for her computer to boot up she looked out of the window. Students were hurrying to lectures, and a traffic warden was already patrolling cars parked on the Broad.

She turned back to her computer and was soon absorbed in sales figures while the volunteers got on with serving customers and checking stock.

'The post has arrived.'

'Thank you, Mary.' Lisa smiled as she took a bundle of envelopes from a small grey-haired woman.

'How's your mother today?'

'She was fine this morning,' Lisa said with forced cheerfulness.

Mary nodded sympathetically as Lisa flicked through the envelopes.

'There's one with a Nigerian stamp. Oh, it's from Sam.'

'The student who stayed with you?' Mary's voice had a soft Oxfordshire burr.

'Yes.' Lisa scanned the letter. 'Oh dear!' she said as Mary was leaving the room.

'Not bad news?'

'His father died of a heart attack.' Lisa frowned. 'And Sam didn't get back in time.'

'I'm sorry for your friend.' Mary touched Lisa lightly on the shoulder as she left.

Lisa glanced across at Trinity College, unmoved by the colourful hanging baskets and the multi-lingual exclamations of delight from tourists.

Since her mother's death on New Year's Day, she had felt suspended in time. She had the support of friends and colleagues, but she came from a small family and her relatives were all distant. Throughout the summer she had felt weighed down by loss. Previously she had enjoyed watching graduates throwing their caps in the air when they spilled onto the Broad fresh from receiving their degrees. But now the hugs from proud parents were too painful, and she kept the window firmly shut.

The autumn air was chilly as Lisa cycled home through St Giles.

'Watch where you're going!' She rang her bell and swerved to avoid a fresh-faced student wobbling on his bike as he gazed up at the historic buildings. She pedalled furiously, angry with herself for shouting but resenting the optimism of the undergraduates teeming into Oxford for the start of Michaelmas term.

Her heart was palpitating by the time she reached the little terraced house which she had shared with her mother and which was now hers. As she was locking her bike she noticed a parcel tucked behind the recycling box, and her mood lightened when she saw the Nigerian stamps.

She took the package into the kitchen and opened it carefully. Inside was a bronze mask about the size of her palm. The eyes were hollowed and the lips had been fashioned so that they looked soft despite the hardness of the metal. The nose was broad and the nostrils flared. The full cheeks had cicitrations similar to those Lisa had noticed on Sam's face.

Still holding the bronze, Lisa tore open the envelope and read Sam's letter. He said he was back in his village making preparations for the wake. The mask was the last thing his father had made before he died and he wanted Lisa to have it as a memento of the weekend he had spent in Oxford and as his tribute to her mother.

Tears ran down her cheeks as she placed the mask on the

table, but she brushed them aside and determinedly chopped vegetables for a stir-fry. As she cooked, her eyes were drawn to the mask and she picked it up, cradling it in her palm. She kept it by her plate as she ate, occasionally tracing the outline of the features with her finger.

Lisa took the mask into the sitting room and wondered whether to light the fire. Instead she slumped onto the settee and switched on the television, flicking channels till she found a travel programme about Africa and, soothed by the sonorous commentary, drifted off to sleep. She woke to the sound of canned laughter and felt a spasm of pain around her heart. She shuddered and stood up, the mask now heavy in her hand. Her mouth felt dry and she walked towards the kitchen breathing rapidly. Another spasm gripped her and, clutching her chest, she turned, dropping the mask into the fireplace. It lay in the grate almost hidden in the cold ashes. Lisa touched her forehead and was surprised to find herself drenched in sweat. She glanced at the telephone, wondering if she should call anyone, but decided she was simply over-tired and would have an early night.

She dreamt of an unfamiliar face, half-hidden behind a waterfall dappled by sunlight, and felt a great tiredness as strange voices whispered in the shadows.

It was dawn when she sat bolt upright, suddenly wide awake. She hurried downstairs to the sitting room and started scrabbling in the fireplace. Her heart began to pound when she saw the bronze face in the ashes. She picked it up, raising a cloud of dust. Hesitantly, she studied the mask. Its features were blurred with ash. She blew away the dust from around the eyes, then started on the nose, giving short quick breaths. As specks rose from the nostrils she almost felt as if she were giving the kiss of life. When she looked up at the mantelpiece she saw the smiling photo of her mother and carefully put the mask on the table.

Lisa turned on the radio and switched on the lights. By the time she was ready to leave for work she had thoroughly cleaned the kitchen and felt able to face the day. She wheeled her bike down the garden path, then stopped, certain she had forgotten something. She went back into the house and looked around the living room. The mask lay on the table and, scarcely aware what she was doing, she stuffed it in her bag.

Mary put her head round the office door. 'Good morning, Lisa. How are you today?'

Lisa opened her mouth to say she was fine then pressed her hand on her chest as she was seized by another spasm.

'Are you all right?' Mary's face was full of concern.

'I'm fine. Just a touch of indigestion.'

'I'll get a glass of water.'

When Mary returned Lisa was holding the mask.

'What a beautiful piece,' Mary said. 'Where did it come from?'

'Sam sent it to me. His father made it.' She stroked the cheeks, then gasped and grimaced in pain.

'Lisa, you're not well.' Mary handed her the glass. 'How long has this been going on?'

Still holding the mask, Lisa sipped the water. She looked across to Trinity College gardens, resplendent in shades of autumn, and remembered Sam's visit nearly a year ago. 'It only started yesterday.' She frowned. 'After I opened the parcel.'

Mary's face was serious. 'May I look at the mask?'

Lisa hesitated, then reluctantly handed her the bronze.

Mary sat down. 'Thank you.' Her expression was unfathomable as she studied it: then her eyes closed. Lisa, confused, wondered if she had fallen asleep.

'I can hear running water,' Mary said. 'There is a compound surrounded by a high cactus hedge. In the compound are several huts. There is an old man sitting outside the largest hut. He is making something... ' Her voice trailed off and she winced sharply. She shook herself, screwed up her face in concentration and continued.

'The old man is sick. I can see a shadow over his head. I get the impression that he is working against time, that there is something he wants to finish before he goes.'

The room was quiet as Mary sat silent for few minutes longer. Then she opened her eyes and looked into Lisa's wondering face.

'Sam told me his family have a cactus hedge round their compound,' Lisa said.

'And I remember you saying that his father died?'

'Yes, almost a year ago, of a heart attack. Sam said the mask was the last thing he made.'

'A heart attack, yes I can feel it. And now this poor troubled soul is imprisoned in his craft and struggling to get back to his native land.'

'I don't understand.' Lisa stared at the woman in front of her, who seemed too ordinary to have this sort of vision. Her mind wandered back to a conversation with Sam. '...Sometimes a soul has difficulty getting to the other side, but when a wake is held... '

'The wake!' Lisa held out her hand for the mask. 'Perhaps it needs to be back for the wake.'

Mary nodded. 'I think it's sending you a message.'

'What should I do?'

'Maybe you should send it back.'

'I'll think about it.'

'Do you think I'm doing the right thing?' Lisa asked as she and Mary joined the queue at the post office.

'I'm sure you are.'

'Cashier number five, please!'

Lisa shuffled to the counter. 'This parcel is very heavy,' she said, cradling it in her arms.

'Put it on the scales, please.'

Lisa's hand trembled as she put it down.

The cashier gave her a strange look. 'It's less than a kilo.'

'Is that all?' Lisa counted out the money.

'It's on its way now,' she said quietly as they went out into St Aldate's.

Lisa was very tired for the next few days, but the chest pains had gone and she felt less angry when she saw people enjoying themselves.

A week after she had posted the mask, she heard the sound

of drums outside the shop. She looked out of the window, but there were only the usual parked cars, bicycles and a tourist bus. She looked again and felt herself gathered up among a throng of brightly clad people singing and dancing to the beat of drums. Her office was filled with tropical heat and fragrant smells.

The door opened and she turned startled eyes towards the intruder.

'What's the matter? You look as if you've seen a ghost,' said Mary.

'I think I have,' Lisa said simply.

She looked out of the window again. The scene returned to normal but the sun had come out and for an instant she saw her mother's face.

And for the first time in months she felt at peace and ready to embrace her future.

THE NIGHT OF THE NEWTS

RADMILA MAY

On Sunday night there were five of us - four by Monday - in Botley Old Hall, cut off by the snow: but it wasn't that which prevented us from leaving. Let me explain.

'You're late,' my Aunt Rose had said when I arrived on Friday afternoon. I wasn't, but there was no point arguing. In reality I was doing her a favour, giving up my weekend so I could skivvy at one of her literary gatherings, while she played the woman of letters.

'Shall I start?' I said.

My aunt sniffed. 'Not cooking. Not after last time. I've hired a chef. You make yourself useful. Peel the potatoes, lay the table. When the first guests arrive, put on a presentable dress - if you've got one - and hand round drinks. I suppose I'd better let you serve the meal. Try not to drop dishes in the guests' laps.'

'It only happened once,' I said humbly.

It wasn't easy to determine whether the chef was a young man or a young woman. Clothes and hair are so ambiguous, these days, and as for make-up... but on closer inspection, I could see very faint designer stubble. And the voice was unmistakeably male.

'Hullo, dear, I'm Shane.'

I introduced myself and added that I was there to help in the kitchen.

'That's nice, dear. I could do with a hand. That aunt of yours, what a wicked tongue. She's a real tartar.'

'That's just her way,' I said. I never speak ill of anyone.

Shane asked me about the house. 'Lovely place. Real style. All those beams and mullioned windows. And a view of Oxford's dreaming spires. Bags of money, anyhow. How long's her old man been dead?'

'Some time,' I said.

He winked. 'Maybe she bit his head off once too often. Well, I can tell you one thing. She's thinking of marrying again.'

I was astonished. Aunt Rose had always insisted that she much preferred the single state.

'Straight up,' Shane said. 'I overheard her on the telephone. She's got two gents dangling. Says she'll make up her mind by Sunday night. So you and me can keep our eyes open this weekend. Run a little book perhaps.'

I don't approve of gambling. But Shane's remarks certainly gave me cause for thought.

Over the weekend I spent my time waiting on the guests or clearing up after them. My aunt had a sharp eye as well as a sharp tongue and called me back several times to re-do some task which I had thought finished.

'Why do it?' Shane asked. 'What's in it for you?'

'I like to serve,' I murmured.

He rolled his eyes. 'Sooner you than me.'

We did manage the odd chat over snatched cups of tea about which of the male guests might be my aunt's suitors. But it was difficult to tell; she wriggled and pouted and fluttered her eyelashes girlishly at them all. So inappropriate in such a heavy woman. Two men, however, were noticeably attentive: Sir Trooby Mowles, a backbench MP, and Erik Dale, a retired businessman.

I ventured my suspicions to Shane while he prepared canapés.

His eyes brightened. 'Which one's the favourite? What do you reckon the odds are? Why don't you chat them up while you're circulating the drinks?'

I did try. But I was caught by the only woman guest, a thin angular poetess in flowing garments.

'I do feel poetry must be deeply personal.' She clutched at the draperies across her non-existent bosom. 'I like to celebrate the beautiful things in life. But today attitudes are so Philistine, so Neanderthal.'

I ventured to tell her about my own effort, a verse drama about Martin Luther called *From Oblivion to Eternity*. But my aunt intervened. 'More of your nonsense, I suppose. Nobody wants to hear it.'

Shane, however, was interested so after dinner I read him some extracts.

'It's lovely, dear. I like the beginning where Luther comes up the Rhine in a boat and says, "Ho, varlets." Real class, that. I used to tread the boards myself, you know, Shakespeare, rep, the classics.'

We were, I confess, rather tiddly by that time. Shane had opened a bottle of Sauternes - 'can't stand all that claret and burgundy they're drinking, gives me a terrible head' - and then another. I rarely drink but after the stressful day the wine was pleasantly relaxing. It was gone midnight when I crept up the stairs to my attic bedroom - unheated, of course - but the guests were, to judge from the noise, still imbibing. Outside the window a few snowflakes drifted past.

By lunchtime on Sunday, it was snowing heavily. Some guests decided to leave early. I mentioned to my aunt that perhaps I should also depart. 'Good God, no,' she said. 'Sir Trooby and Mr Dale are staying another night. I shall need you.'

Shane grumbled. 'I've had enough of this place. But if the old bat coughs up for the extra time I might as well. There's some stewing steak so I can do a nice boeuf bourguignon. I expect she'll make up her mind between the two of them tonight. I wonder which.'

I wondered too.

It was a surprise to be invited to dine with my aunt and the two remaining guests.

'Sooner you than me. Fancy more Sauternes?' Shane offered.

'How kind,' I said, 'but please don't trouble yourself. I've found this one.'

He glanced at the label. 'Never heard of it. I'll stick to the Sauternes. Think of me when you're dining with the high and mighty.'

The meal was unexpectedly pleasant. The boeuf bourguignon was delicious, the claret flowed, Sir Trooby and Erik were charming and even my aunt mellowed slightly. When I took the dirty dishes out to the kitchen, I said to Shane, 'Don't bother about these. I'll put them in the dishwasher.'

He shrugged. 'As you choose. I'm well stuck in.' He brandished his bottle. 'Plenty more where this came from. More of your tipple, dear? Pass your glass.'

After dinner, my aunt, Sir Trooby and Erik retired to the library. I joined them and Aunt Rose ordered me to fill up everyone's glasses, whisky for the two men, brandy for herself.

Sir Trooby and my aunt were deep in conversation so I chose an armchair beside Erik. He murmured, 'Your aunt is a wonderful woman. But I'm afraid she doesn't think much of my literary efforts.' He produced a sheaf of grubby typescript from his pocket. 'Would you like - ?'

'Of course,' I said.

It is not my place to criticise but I must admit I found Erik's writing less than fascinating. It was the first chapter of a novel about a young man of deep sensitivity who was misunderstood by everyone around him. Erik had a soft Scottish voice, and occasionally paused to say, 'Shall I go on?' before, without waiting for a reply, launching into a further instalment. From time to time I refilled all the glasses. At one point Erik offered me some brandy.

'Just a teeny tiny one,' I said. 'The room seems to be going round and round. And I've still got some of the wine I was drinking at dinner. I'm afraid it's my second bottle. Or is my third? How awful, I've lost count.' I giggled tipsily.

He patted my hand. 'Don't worry, my dear. You are a womanly woman.' The phrase was familiar. I rather thought he had used it of his hero's mother. Several times.

We were interrupted by a bang at the door. It was Shane, clutching a bottle. 'I want my money,' he announced. 'I've had enough of this piss-awful place.' I suspect the Sauternes prompted the outburst.

'You'll have to wait,' my aunt snapped back. 'You'll be paid tomorrow morning.'

'I'll be paid now,' he shouted. 'I'm bloody tired and bloody fed up.'

She got up and stalked out. 'Come into the study. I suppose you want cash.'

Shane followed her and I followed him. In the hall I said, 'Aunt Rose. Is there anything I can do?'

She turned on me. 'When I want you I'll tell you.'

I returned to the library. Sir Trooby was apparently asleep but Erik looked up eagerly. He had taken a fresh - though no cleaner - batch of typescript from somewhere about his person. I thought I had heard quite enough. 'It's very - Scandinavian,' I said.

He smirked triumphantly 'You guessed! I am indeed of Viking stock!' He was a small man, fat and soft looking, with large pale eyes and a mass of grey curls. He didn't look at all like Erik Bloodaxe or Harald Bluetooth.

'My ancestors were Norse raiders. Berserkers,' he announced proudly. 'They would go naked into battle.' The picture he conjured up was not pretty.

I smiled and offered him another whisky.

'More of the amber nectar? Fit for Valhalla? You are indeed a temptress.'

As I refilled his glass, voices were raised outside the library. Then a door slammed. 'Excuse me,' I said.

Shane was in the hall, waving his bottle. 'Rotten old cow. She's underpaid me. Told me to take the money and go. I ask you, how can I? It's snowing fit to bust. And to tell you the truth, I don't feel up to it.' He put the bottle to his lips, swallowed and sagged at the knees. Then he grabbed at my shoulder to stop himself from falling. 'You've been at the bottle too, dear. Naughty old thing. Frankly, my dear, everyone's as - '

I can't bring myself to say what he said next. So vulgar, so unrefined. Something to do with newts and their alcoholic intake.

'You should lie down,' I said. 'There's a sofa in the cloakroom. Why don't you flop down on that and sleep until morning?'

'Sleep? Sleep? Don' wanna sleep. Wan' another drink, wan' my money. Old bag!' he shouted. 'I'll get you, see if I don't.'

'In the morning,' I said, propelling him into the cloakroom and pushing him onto the sofa. 'You'll feel so much better.'

He was already snoring. I arranged a few coats over his recumbent body and left him to sleep off his excesses.

In the study my aunt was slumped in an armchair with a full glass of brandy in one hand and a nearly empty bottle of brandy on a table nearby.

'What do you want?' she said in a voice so slurred I could barely understand her.

'Dear aunt,' I said. 'Can I assist?'

She told me in no uncertain terms just what to do, and gulped down her drink. Her head fell back, her eyes closed. I took a deep breath, turned off the light, and closed the door on her slumbers.

Back in the library, Erik and Sir Trooby were now on their feet, facing each other like angry but decrepit old dogs.

'You blackguard,' Erik was shouting. 'You creep in behind my back. How dare you?' He approached Sir Trooby, hand raised as if to strike him. I stepped between them.

'What's going on?' I said.

'You may well ask. Betrayal! All those years of devotion to your aunt, gone for nothing.' Erik sounded very drunk and slightly tearful.

I turned to Sir Trooby. 'Do you know - '

Erik pushed me aside. 'Don't listen to that viper!'

Sir Trooby said, 'I say, old chap - '

Erik pushed me aside and aimed a swipe at Sir Trooby. 'I'll teach you!'

'Oh, please,' I begged. 'He's such an old man.'

'Not that old, dear lady,' Sir Trooby said, sidestepping neatly.

Erik staggered and fell across the hearthrug.

'My God!' I cried, and knelt to feel his pulse.

'Don't you bother about him,' said Sir Trooby. 'He's all right. Out cold but he'll be fine in the morning. If you could just help me back to my chair - thank you, m'dear - and top up my glass - how kind - and one for yourself.'

I poured out one more whisky. 'I'll go on with the wine I was drinking at dinner,' I said. 'There's just enough for another glass. And I do really think I've had enough. I feel just a wee bit tiddly.'

'Not used to alcohol?'

'Not really,' I said. 'Oh, dear, your glass is empty. More?'

'Thank you, m'dear. And then let us drink a toast.'

'A toast?'

'To your aunt. Who has made me the happiest man in England.'

'You don't mean - are congratulations in order?'

'They are indeed. Your Aunt Rose and I have agreed to tie the knot. She's a wonderful, wonderful woman,' he went on, and held his glass out for another refill. 'Such a delicate, tender little flower. She needs to be cherished. She is a rich woman, you know. She has a great deal of property, not just this house but investments as well. She should have someone to look after all that.'

'I'm sure you're just the man,' I said. 'Your glass needs topping up.'

'Just one more, m'dear. That's it, that's splendid.' He downed the tumbler's contents in one gulp. 'Such a wonderful, wonderful wo - ' His eyes closed. He began to snore.

I turned out all the lights except for a small lamp in one corner of the room. Then I took a clean glass from the sideboard, poured a good measure of brandy for myself, and sat staring into the fireplace.

When I awoke next morning my head was throbbing and there seemed to be pandemonium inside it. Then I realised that the noise was coming from downstairs. In the hall all was confusion. Shane was sobbing and yelling, Erik was moaning loudly and Sir Trooby was shouting.

'She's dead, she's dead,' Shane wailed, mascara-streaked tears running down the designer stubble. 'In the sitting room. I found her. It was horrible, horrible.'

I turned to Sir Trooby. 'What is he talking about?'

'Terrible news, m'dear. You must brace yourself. Your aunt - I can hardly bear to talk about it. Only yesterday she promised to be mine and now - and now - '

'Her throat's been cut,' Shane bawled. 'Blood everywhere.'

I took a deep breath and walked into the sitting room. There, where I had last seen her, was my aunt. The brandy bottle was empty. So was her glass.

Across my aunt's throat was a deep gash. The front of her dress and the arms and seat of the chair were soaked in blood. More blood was in a pool before her feet. In it there lay a kitchen knife.

She was, without a doubt, dead. And, without a doubt, by the hand of a murderer.

I went back into the hall. Shane threw himself on his knees and clutched at my dress. 'See the chip on the handle of the knife? It's the one I used to cut up the beef for the boeuf bourguignon.'

'We should call the police,' I said. 'Someone must have broken in while we were all asleep - '

I was interrupted by the sound of retching. Erik was being sick into the umbrella stand. Then he said, his face ghastly, 'It was snowing last night. Now it's stopped. I've just looked. There are no tracks. It must have been... one of us.'

There was a long, long silence.

'Impossible,' Sir Trooby whispered. 'We were - we couldn't have - after the amount we had to drink last night we couldn't possibly have done anything. We were all paralytic. Out cold. I know I was. And you - ' he turned to me ' - you were, too.'

I nodded. 'I can't remember anything from last night. Nothing at all.'

'Nor me,' said Erik. 'When I came to this morning I was lying face down on the hearthrug with no idea how I'd got there.'

There was a low moan from Shane. 'We were all pissed. Pissed as newts.'

I have to put the blame on someone - "finger", I believe, is the correct term. Such a pity it has to be Shane. Of the three of them he was the most entertaining. And the only one to see the true merit of *From Oblivion to Eternity*. But the knife lying in the pool of blood at my aunt's feet, the knife that he used for the boeuf bourguignon, has his fingerprints. And no one else's.

Of course, it wasn't the knife I actually used when I went back into the sitting room to deal with Aunt Rose. That was another knife, which I had taken from the kitchen. I removed my outer garments to avoid incriminating bloodstains. Then I cut her throat. Not a pleasant job but I steeled myself to it. Then I scrubbed and scoured that knife and returned it to its proper place. After that, using a pair of kitchen tongs, I picked up Shane's unwashed knife and dropped it at my aunt's feet. Then I put on my clothes again. Nowadays one has to be very careful. Those forensic science TV series - *CSI, Silent Witness, Waking the Dead* - are so informative. Finally, I placed all the empty bottles in the recycling box so kindly provided by the council and always collected early on Monday morning. That was an essential feature of my plan. Thankfully, the recycling lorry has already been and gone, preceding the police whose sirens are now audible.

The experts will undoubtedly identify Shane's fingerprints on the knife. And we all heard him quarrelling with my aunt, and about money too. That should be enough to establish motive.

My motive, of course, is also money. I knew that my aunt had never made a will. Not uncommon, I understand, even among the wealthy. All her property comes to me as her next-of-kin. But all would have been different had she married Sir Trooby; he would have got everything. Unjust, don't you think?

Now I can live in Botley Old Hall and underwrite a production of From Oblivion to Eternity. T.S. Eliot's *Murder in the Cathedral* had its premiere in Canterbury Cathedral: *From Oblivion to Eternity* should be first staged here at Christ Church Cathedral in Oxford.

But, you ask, how was I able to perform the dreadful deed? Surely I was as incapable as the others? All that wine, and then the brandy? How could I, so unaccustomed to alcoholic beverages, plan and execute this complicated plan so efficiently?

Let me explain. It is true that we were all in that newt-like condition which Shane so vulgarly described. But in my case, it wasn't until after I had disposed of my aunt that I made myself well and truly drunk on brandy while Sir Trooby snored in the armchair and Erik grunted and snuffled on the hearthrug and poor Shane lay comatose in the cloakroom. I needed it, I can tell you. Murder isn't something one does every day.

But the wine? Two bottles? Three?

Ah, that is the point. You may not be familiar with that particular brand of sweet - not to say sickly - wine I was imbibing. Actually, it was non-alcoholic. Completely, totally, absolutely non-alcoholic.

It would be difficult for anyone, even a newt, to get pissed on it.

THE PLAY'S THE THING

SYLVIA VETTA

One balmy evening during the previous summer, when the rain briefly ceased, Ben's girlfriend had dragged him to Headington Hill Park to see *Romeo and Juliet*. That was his first experience of Shakespeare in performance. The consequences had been delicious: the taste of Chris's tears, when she responded to him, like melting butter.

This year the same company, Creation Theatre, was performing *Hamlet*, and his girlfriend was still into literature and art. Ben was aware that the play was set in a castle - this performance would be, appropriately, at the recently redeveloped Oxford Castle - and could even quote one line from it: "To be or not to be, that is the question".

But that dilemma was not for him. Just twenty-two and in his final year at Oxford Brookes, he was expected to get a first in Economics. A comfortable childhood lay behind him. He was handsome, popular with his fellow students, and his future with Chris seemed full of promise and delight. Ben took out his mobile to text her about Hamlet. 'Yes pls' came the reply, so he booked two seats for a matinée performance.

In three weeks, his finals would be over and he could look forward to a break with Chris in Thailand before starting on his PGCE. Needing cash for the holiday, he organised a summer job working for a restaurant in the Golden Cross.

'Is that some kind of coincidence?' said Chris on hearing his news. 'Some scholars think the first performance of Hamlet took place in the courtyard of the Golden Cross. Shakespeare came to Oxford and probably slept in the inn overlooking it. I've heard that his bedroom is part of the restaurant. Let's go for a meal tonight and take a look.'

After some special pleading from Chris they were shown to a table in the otherwise-deserted side room. 'Look, over there' cried an enthusiastic Chris, 'Elizabethan wall-paintings!' Maybe the slot machine was to blame, but Ben's imagination failed to visualize Shakespeare sitting in that very place. He didn't like to own up to Chris. 'Was this really his bedroom? Poor old bard,' remarked Ben. 'Coming back to haunt the place and finding it full of pizza.' He felt as if he could drown himself in Chris's tender brown eyes. 'Without you, I don't suppose I would be going to see *Hamlet*. Maybe old Will isn't relevant any more.'

'You'd be surprised,' said Chris.

She was doing a nursing degree, and, as Ben walked back with her to her hall of residence in Cheney Lane, their talk was more Shakespearean than Ben realised - "If music be the food of love", washed up on the beach in Phuket.

The day after Ben's final exams began, there was a knock on the door of his shared house in Howard Street. His mate, Rajiv, opened the door to two police officers, who asked for Ben. Rajiv showed them into the sitting room and apologised for the leftovers. They seemed surreal in their immaculate uniforms amid the sordid student chaos: and Ben could not believe what he was hearing. His father was assumed dead; his jacket, shoes and backpack discovered on Parr Sands, where the current was treacherous.

'It was a strange time to go swimming,' they said, 'a really rough night.'

Ben couldn't take it in. Why hadn't his mother told him? Why was he hearing this from the police?

One of the police officers explained. 'I am sorry, Mr Butcher, to have to break the news like this, but we are trying to contact your mother. The community policeman called at the house last night but she wasn't there. Do you know where we can find her?'

Ben took out his mobile and scrolled down to "Home". After what felt like a thousand rings, the answering machine clicked in. The certainties in Ben's world were collapsing even as he blinked. His parents lived not far away, in the village of Uffington, set beneath the ancient White Horse carved into the hillside. The police drove him there and the journey, a mere twenty-five minutes of finger-twisting tension, felt interminable. As they passed St Mary's Church, the village seemed unchanged. The playing field echoed with memories of football: his father cheering, and his mother bringing on the half-time oranges. The sun shone brightly on the house he called home, so why was his heart shivering?

On opening the front door, he was surprised to see that everything looked, well... normal.

'Mum? Mum, where are you? It's me,' he called, running up the stairs and then opening all the doors. There was no sign of her. He looked in his parents' bedroom and opened the wardrobe doors. Lots of his mother's clothes were missing. Her suitcase - didn't she keep it on top of the wardrobe? But that was gone too. The kind WPC saw how agitated he was and suggested they sit down and have a coffee.

'Is there anyone you can ring to be with you? No brothers or sisters?' Ben shook his head. 'Aunts, uncles?'

Ben still shook his head. 'Aunt Joan lives in Spain and my father's brother James has just retired and is on a round-the-world cruise. '

'Friends?'

'Can you take me back to Oxford?'

The WPC urged him to think of the names of any relations and friends of his parents. Ben looked in the drawer in the hall table but the address book was missing, so he noted all the regular numbers saved on the telephone, added his parent's mobile numbers and, his hand shaking, gave the list to the WPC, who then asked him if they could take a look round.

Ben nodded, and escaped into the garden, where he paced up and down for what seemed like hours, looking angrily at the birds singing as if nothing had happened.

He spent the next day e-mailing and phoning anyone who knew his parents, but they were as shocked as he was: his parents' behaviour seemed so out of character. Fighting back tears and not knowing what to do, he ran to Iffley Lock. But the sight of the usually tranquil river hurtling noisily through the weir unsettled him: rivers, ponds, oceans, they were all water you could drown in.

Back at the flat Rajiv, waiting with Chris, looked up in concern when Ben came in. 'Any luck?'

Ben shook his head.

'I wish we had some news,' Rajiv said, 'but the only call was from Dr. Farr asking why you hadn't turned up for your exam. I called Chris and she handled it.' He seemed at a loss for words after that, but eventually said, 'Maybe your mum went looking for your dad. She probably didn't want to worry you, so close to finals.'

Chris agreed. 'We can't even be certain your father is dead, can we? After all, no one has found a body.'

Ben erupted, glaring. 'Stop it. Stop trying to comfort me, pretending everything is all right when it isn't.' He walked out, slammed the door and headed for the Bullingdon Arms. Chris burst into tears: Rajiv turned to her and said, 'I'm sure he doesn't mean it. I don't know how I can help - but I won't let him drink alone.'

Ten minutes later Rajiv pulled up a chair next to Ben, saying 'What can I get you?'

'Pint.' Ben said little else, but after half an hour sitting with his friend, appeared less agitated.

'Can I do anything?' asked Rajiv.

Ben thought about it.

'Can you tell the Uni - tell them I can't concentrate. I don't know where to look for her but - I can't get it out of my head. I can't think exams.'

The following Thursday, at noon, Ben stretched out a weary hand to answer the phone. It was the WPC who had driven him to Uffington. She had kept in touch with him, prodding memories that might help trace his mother. It was kind of her, because adult missing persons were not a high priority. Her voice sounded more upbeat.

'Ben, do you remember telling me about your mum and dad's favourite holiday destination? You said they often took you to Looe in Cornwall, so we contacted the local police. We told them how you all enjoyed competitions skimming stones and hunting for shells and crabs on West Looe beach. Well, they found your mother in the Hannafore Point Hotel, overlooking it. We have brought her back to Oxford but, just for the time being, she is in the Warneford Hospital. The doctors say she was suffering from temporary amnesia. You can see her, but they want you to go a bit easy. Be careful not to upset her.'

Ben cycled up Divinity Road to the hospital. He was anxious walking in, wondering if his mother might not remember him. When he asked to see Mrs Sarah Butcher, the nurse wanted to stop and talk to him, but he couldn't wait to see his mother again. When he did, tears choked him. After watching the hugs and the loving looks, the nurse said it was OK for them to go for a walk in Warneford Meadow.

Out in the sunshine, Ben asked, 'How are you, Mum? Do you remember driving down to Looe?'

His mother gave a weak smile. 'I do remember leaving, but nothing after that.'

Ben put his arm around her and said, 'You don't realise how good it is to have you back. I am sorry, Mum, I hope I haven't let you down. I didn't do my last exams. After the news about Dad - I still can't really believe it.'

Sarah sighed. 'You do know that your dad and I adore you.' She began to cry, and Ben held her tighter. 'I just couldn't bring myself to tell you,' she said.

Pulling away, he said, 'Tell me what, mum?'

She didn't answer immediately: then, slowly, she said, 'When you left for University - your dad and I were alone. We did care about each other, but, somehow - we gradually just stopped being married... and I felt so lonely... ' Her eyes misted over. 'I am sorry now, but it just sort of happened. Do you remember Roger, from our badminton club? He asked me out - I'm not sure why - but I couldn't bring myself to have a proper affair, not while I was still married. So I told your father I wanted a divorce. He stormed out of the house, just like that, without a word, and that was the last I saw of him - please don't hate me, Ben, I couldn't bear it.' She wept. 'I didn't mean it to end like this. I am so sorry, Ben. Your father and I love you so much. Neither of us wanted to hurt you. It all happened so suddenly.'

Ben pushed his mother away. 'How could you? A slime-ball like Roger! I don't want to see him, not ever. I just don't want to see you together knowing - it would be like - like meeting my father's murderer.'

'Ben,' cried Sarah. 'How can you say that? They - they don't know for sure that John is dead... they never found him... the rest of his clothes... surely there is still hope, Ben.'

'No,' Ben said: and, ignoring her pleading, he turned and walked unsteadily away, leaving her swaying and fragile as the tall dried grass, ghostly in the meadow.

As soon as Ben left for the Warneford, Rajiv had phoned Chris with the news, so they were both waiting for him. As he walked through the door Chris ran towards him saying, 'What wonderful news! How is your m- ?'

Ben's expression cut her short. He pushed past them. 'I'll tell you later,' he said, and shut himself in his room. But "later" didn't happen.

Ben didn't return to the hospital: Rajiv and Chris thought that perhaps Sarah's amnesia meant she hadn't known him. As the days passed, when Ben wasn't working at the Golden Cross, Rajiv kept him company with games on the Wii, or bar billiards with friends at The Isis. Still Ben never mentioned his mother. He didn't even ring Chris: but, eventually, she rang him.

'Are we still seeing *Hamlet* tomorrow afternoon? It would be a pity to waste those tickets. Are you up for going, Ben?'

It dawned on Ben that he had not seen Chris for days. Was it even weeks? No, surely not - so he agreed. But it was with reluctance that he took his seat in the open-air theatre created, for the summer, in the castle grounds. What else could he do? Better watch *Hamlet* than try to drown his sorrows at the pub.

They sat in silence. The first scene opened with the officers of the guard walking on the wall of the castle mound, but Ben's mind was elsewhere. Then the ghost appeared. Ben let out a sudden gasp. The actor looked every inch like his father. He could easily be a twin. How could this be happening? Chris understood, and put out a hand to steady him, but Ben brushed it aside.

As the play went on he identified more and more with Hamlet, Prince of Denmark. He felt for his dilemma with a depth of understanding that defied reason. Ben clenched his fists when Hamlet was unkindly dismissive of Ophelia. With a jolt he recognised himself. He had been like that with Chris ever since the day he received news of his father's disappearance. When Ophelia drowned, he felt needles in his eyes but pushed away his emotions. It was only a play, for god's sake.

Then Gertrude looked at her son, with the same expression on her face that Sarah had worn when she gazed at Ben through the grass in the meadow. "Oh Hamlet, thou has cleft my heart in twain."

Surveying the final scene, the stage strewn with bodies of the unnecessary dead, Ben felt that somehow Hamlet's mental turmoil and his indecision had led to a massacre of innocence. Surely he wasn't really cruel? How had it happened?

'I am no longer me,' Ben thought. 'It is as if another man, a careless unkind soul, has taken me over.'

He sat through the applause, hardly moving. Then, as the audience began to leave, he pushed through the crowds, and rushed up to a stage hand. 'The ghost,' Ben said, to a startled and wary young man. 'The actor who played the ghost, what's his name?'

'Sorry, mate, I don't know - I'm only working here for a week. It'll be in the programme.'

Ben made his way back to an anxious-looking Chris. 'What's the matter, Ben?'

'Nothing,' he said, bending down to pick up an abandoned and trampled programme. He thought for a moment. 'I hope.'

When they reached South Park, Ben pulled Chris close for the first time in weeks and wept through his kisses. 'I've seen myself at last. Through someone else's eyes. Sorry, honey - I've been such an idiot. Will you come with me to see my Mum - right now?'

JUST KEEP GOING

GINA CLAYE

Sally hadn't heard him arrive; the carpet in the drawing room at the Randolph Hotel muffled all footsteps. She pushed the draft for his new brochure back in her bag. She'd finish correcting it tomorrow.

'You're late. I was beginning to worry about you.'

'Only ten minutes.' Daniel settled his rather bulky figure in the other armchair. 'I'm sorry.'

'Did you have a good journey?' she asked as the waitress put a pot of tea on the table and departed.

'Not bad.'

He looks tired, thought Sally. 'Didn't you have anything to eat on the train? It's a long time, Glasgow to Oxford.'

'I had a bite to eat at twelve but it seems ages ago. A lot has happened.' He glanced at his watch.

'Have a scone. They look delicious.' She was beginning to feel nervous. Why had he suggested they meet here?

'I'd rather have a cup of tea.'

She poured milk into the cups and reached for the teapot. He was looking at her. Had he noticed that she'd dressed up for the occasion? After all, it wasn't every day they had afternoon tea at the Randolph. She handed him a cup and took a scone. 'How did the shoot go?'

'Aaah,' he breathed as he took the cup and leaned back in the armchair. 'It was brilliant. They wanted shots of early morning mists over the loch, sun setting behind the hills, that sort of thing, as well as the usual pics of dining room, bedrooms etc. It took a whole afternoon up on the moors to get a picture of a stag - just as the sun was setting. Perfect.'

'You enjoyed yourself.'

'It was wonderful.'

She felt a pang of envy. Since they'd been together she'd gone to the shoot whenever she could, but she'd had no holiday left to go with him this time.

She took another scone. She really couldn't resist them.

'Why did you suggest afternoon tea?' she asked. 'I could have picked you up at the station and we'd have been home by now. I'm glad you did, though,' she added as she piled cream and plum jam on top.

He hesitated. 'I thought it would be a good idea.'

She waited, her mouth full of delicious scone.

'Yes, you see, there's no easy way of saying this.' He put his cup down on the table. 'I'm not coming home.'

'Not coming home?' she repeated. 'Where are you going?'

'We're…'

'We? Who's we?'

'Well, me and… Marian.'

'Who's Marian?'

'She was with me in Scotland, this week. She's waiting for me.'

'Waiting?'

'Yes, she's having a drink in the Morse Bar.'

'Now?'

'Yes.' He was looking down at the carpet.

'While you're here with me?' She couldn't keep the disbelief, the hurt out of her voice.

'I'm sorry, there's no easy way to do this... and the Randolph Hotel, afternoon tea... I suppose it's my way of saying goodbye.'

'Would you like more hot water?' asked the waitress.

'No thank you,' said Daniel, 'just the bill, please.'

This wasn't happening, she told herself. He couldn't be going, couldn't be leaving her.

'You haven't had a scone,' she blurted out.

'I'm sorry,' said Daniel as he reached into his pocket for his wallet. 'You've been wonderful, doing all the publicity, writing the brochure. You've been a great help. I wouldn't have landed the Glenhall job if it hadn't been for you.'

She wished she'd never heard of Glenhall, never told him about it.

'I knew Marian before I went to Scotland,' he said gently. 'We met here in Oxford.'

'How long have you known her?' Sally demanded.

'Long enough to be sure that it's what we both want,' he

said. 'Three months to be precise. And I am sure, especially after being together for the last few days.

'I'm sorry,' he went on. 'It's totally my fault. I despise myself for doing this to you but I can't help it. And I did need to tell you face to face.'

'What about your things?' she managed.

'I'll come round for them in a few days, when you've had time to... ' He paused, heaved himself out of the armchair and stood looking down at her. 'I'll ring first. I'm sorry, Sally, I really am.' He shrugged his shoulders helplessly and turned away. 'Goodbye.'

He was gone. She sat frozen on the edge of her armchair, every muscle tense. How long she stayed there motionless, until disturbed by the waitress clearing the table, she had no idea. She had to do something. She couldn't stay here. The room was empty apart from a woman reading a book to a little girl with curly hair, and a younger woman cradling a baby. She had to make herself move. It was stuffy in here; she couldn't breathe. She needed a drink. Not in the Morse Bar. She must find somewhere else. She jerked her chair backwards, nearly losing her balance as she did so.

She found herself outside, not really knowing how she'd got there. She turned right; she could get a drink down here. Panting, she hurried down an alley way past a bookshop until she came to the pub. She pushed the door open; it was full of people. She hesitated then walked in; somehow being part of a crowd made her feel safe.

Surprisingly there was no queue at the bar. She bought the first drink that came into her head, a brandy, and perched on the nearest bar stool as all the tables were occupied. She took a sip but it did nothing to calm her; her heart was racing. Slowly she became aware of a man standing at a microphone speaking. She caught the words "book launch".

Her glass was empty. She couldn't remember finishing her drink. She couldn't think why, but she knew she had to go. Outside she made for the main street, the words "just keep going" ringing in her head. A family of Japanese tourists came out of the bookshop and overtook her. Without thinking, her head pounding, she followed them. Jostled by the stream of shoppers and sightseers, she allowed herself to be carried forward, on and on. She had no idea what time it was. Late afternoon, perhaps? Some of the shops had already closed. Her breath came in short gasps. She must keep going; where didn't matter. A number of people were crossing the road; she was swept along with them, seemed to have no will of her own. Her mind was racing. He'd left her; he'd gone; it was just like Mark all over again. After the children had left home he'd gone too. She'd spent her life looking after the family and helping him run the art gallery. She felt the familiar fear rising - what was she going to do without Daniel? What was she going to do now she was on her own?

'I'm so sorry.' The voice was American. 'I guess I wasn't looking where I was going. Are you OK?'

Sally stared at her blankly, winded by the contact. 'I'm all right, thank you, really I am,' she managed. The woman looked unconvinced, but was with a group, and hurried on.

But it had brought her up short. She stood there, fists clenching and unclenching. What was she doing here? She knew she had to keep going, but where?... the car. Where had she left the car? How had she got here? And where was she? Bewildered, she looked around. Opposite was Tom Tower and Christ Church behind it. She stepped into the road and immediately back again as a bus blasted its horn at her. With an effort Sally managed to reach the other side of the road; she passed through the entrance of Christ Church, and hurried across the quad.

Somewhere to sit, somewhere peaceful. Breathless, she reached the door.

'It's all right, no need to hurry. Cathedral time is always five minutes behind ordinary time. You won't be late for Evensong.' The man in the bowler hat was reassuring.

Someone was telling her what to do. She would go to Evensong. She would sit and let it all happen round her.

Inside, the low tones of the organ enveloped her. All was still, the silent stone walls absorbing both music and quiet footfalls. She stopped abruptly, wondering where to sit, and a woman moved forward with a smile to show her to a seat. She sank down gratefully on the wooden bench. She hardly noticed others rising when the choir entered, followed by the clergy.

She sat motionless, heedless of the reverent murmur around her, just grateful for the tranquillity, for the peace, for not having to decide what to do. She became aware of her heartbeat, the rhythm gradually slowing as though settling itself in time to the choir-master's controlled arm movements, the drawn-out harmonies of the choir, the chanting around her. Her breath was quietening now, her muscles beginning to relax, to let go, as though the stillness of the ancient stones was gradually seeping into her bones.

Something familiar was stirring in her consciousness: the choir was singing, something she knew from a long time ago... an anthem... Mozart. At first she sat mesmerized as the strains of the *Ave Verum* washed over her. Then silently she began to sing the alto part, *de Maria Virgine...* She remembered it, after all these years, *pro homine...* and as she mouthed the words, the phrasing came back to her and with it the slow deep breaths that supported the measured tread of the music, *in mortis examine...* She felt as though she were breathing properly for the first time in her life.

Evensong had ended. Most of the congregation had gone but she sat there listening to the organ, unwelcome thoughts seeping back. Daniel had left her; she was on her own once more. She didn't want to go home. It would be so lonely. But what else was she to do? She didn't want to walk aimlessly round Oxford, didn't want to just keep going.

Just keep going. She'd heard those words recently. Where had she heard them? The pub... the pub where she'd had that drink. He'd said them, the man at the microphone, Colin somebody, the one who wrote Inspector Morse. It was beginning to come back to her. Something about writing... writing the opening sentence. That was it, something about "if you sit down with a blank sheet of paper determined to write the best possible opening sentence you'll be sitting there for a long time".

Sitting, she was still sitting; the organ had stopped playing. She lifted her bag to her shoulder and got up. More bits were coming back. What else had he said? "Accept that you'll probably write the worst opening sentence that's ever been written and then write the next one and the next and just keep going". She walked slowly towards the door.

Just keep going, those words; they'd been haunting her. He'd been talking about writing a novel... that was it. She'd had an idea for a children's book once - her sketches were in a drawer in the spare bedroom, but she'd never done anything about it.

"If you write a page a day", he'd said, "a year later you'll have 365 pages and that's a book". Had this been the way he'd written his novels? She could never do the same; the familiar feeling of inadequacy rose to the surface. She pushed the thought away. If she'd wanted to, why hadn't she done it? She'd been too busy supporting first her husband then Daniel in their chosen dreams, that's why; she'd lived through them.

What had he said next? Somehow it was important that she remember. She blinked as she came out of the dark of the cathedral into the evening light. Something about changing the opening sentence... "it might be the worst thing ever written; that's all right because you can change it". Change it. She couldn't change the past; she couldn't change what had happened today. She couldn't change the fact that she was on her own.

She pulled herself up short and took a couple of deep breaths. No, she couldn't change the past, but she could take charge of the present. OK, she was on her own; face it, start from there. She would find the car, go home and run a hot bath... first step. Tomorrow she would start again. Maybe she'd get those sketches out... and this time she wouldn't let anything or anybody distract her.

Deep in thought she made her way round the fountain and was startled to see an elderly man ahead stumble and fall. Her immediate instinct was to rush forward and take charge of the situation, but others were running to his aid. She hesitated, then walked resolutely past the little group and across the quad. It was going to be tough; she would miss Daniel like hell, but she wasn't going to let that stop her. 'Thank you,' she breathed as she crossed the cobbles under Tom Tower. 'I'm taking the first step; from now on I'll just keep going.'

THE STUNNER FROM HOLYWELL

MARY CAVANAGH

1957

Ernesto Luigi Polisano (Polly), was an Oxford antiques dealer. Well, not exactly. He was born Ernest Pollard in 1917, the first and only child of a plodding Wiltshire bank clerk, but thought an Italian connection to be more befitting to his image. His image? In his youth a Byronic charmer, with shiny dark curls, drowsy brown eyes that guaranteed seduction, and a gift for lying with a straight face. Thus, between leaving his minor public school, and taking up a place at Exeter College, he adopted his new persona. After scraping a degree in History, and spending an easy war as a stage manager for ENSA (the Entertainments National Service Association), he wheeled and dealed his way into the world of art and antiques, through natural cunning and a sharp brain. Now, at forty years old, he was a tubby little bantam cock, with a sharp reputation for being a "divvy"; one instantly able to recognise a fake from the genuine article.

In the 1950's Oxford town life was slow, friendly and comfortable, with established family businesses, such as Capes haberdashers, Grimbly Hughes grocery store, and Gill's the ironmongers, the mainstay of town trade. On the pen-pushing front accountants, estate agents, and building society managers, seeming to do very little actual work, would fill the pubs at lunchtime, and weave their way back to their offices for a quiet afternoon. At the end of the day, with opening time being 6.00 pm on the dot, the landlords could expect another influx from the "just-a-swift-one-before-I-go-home" crowd of thirsty workers.

The Old Tom in St Aldates was the chosen home of the antique dealers; a mixed bunch ranging from those with haughty, intimidating emporiums on the High Street (polished and expensive) to Sid Sparrow with his cluttered second hand shop in St Thomas's. Polly, however, conducted his business from a shabby former church hall in Walton Street; crammed, disorganised, and smelling of turps and linseed oil. Every evening he pedalled over to The Old Tom, where business dealings were conducted over Morrell's ale, G and T's, and a fug of cigarette smoke. He would enter with a flourish, followed by a loud shout or an operatic song, stopping all conversation and ensuring he was the centre of attention. As both master of ceremonies, and resident comedian, his outrageous personality was dearly loved, but he was highly central to any transaction that required exaggerated age, enhanced provenance, or bare-faced deceit.

One night, with the bar now emptied, he was called over by Sid Sparrow. 'I need a favour, Poll. I've 'ad bad news. Serious bad news. A couple of geezers from the council came round. Listen to this. St Thomas's is coming down. Paradise Square, Pensons Gardens and Church Street all razed to the ground, so my shop's up the spout. None of the 'ouseholders know they're in for compulsory purchase, so they've all got a big shock coming.' He paused to cough and light a Woodbine. 'I've been told to keep my gob shut, so just to make sure I does they've offered me a back 'ander, and a shop on the Cowley Road. I've got six weeks to get out.'

For once Polly was lost for words – not with sympathy for poor old Sid's situation, but with the fact that a serious sea-change was happening in the city, just round the corner, and he'd heard nothing on the grapevine. His little Machiavellian brain immediately registered that most of the rather fine Victorian and Regency houses, poised for the chop, were inhabited by the elderly, and there might be some decent old pieces to be bargained for on the knocker. But he gave his concentration back to Sid. 'That's bloody awful, Sid. Makes you want to weep. What can I do for you?'

'Thing is,' Sid said, 'I'm getting on and I don't think I can be bothered with it all any more.' He pulled on his soggy fag, and removed a sliver of tobacco from his lip. 'I've just done two 'ouse clearances and the sheds out the back are full to bursting. There's some decent bits and bobs, and the usual old rubbish, but I need it shifting PDQ. Do you think you could come down and see if there's anything that cuts the mustard? I'll go 'alves with you on anything that'll get over three quid.'

'Sounds like a good deal, Sid. Glad to oblige.'

'You're a mate.'

'Just after eleven tomorrow OK?'

1857

St. Helen's Passage, the ancient slype that led off Holywell, afforded no more room than the breadth of a man's shoulders, and wafted the odour of the farmyard. Gabriel knocked on the shabby door with his knuckles, and it was opened by a gentle looking old lady. Behind her stood Jane, her tall, stately daughter. 'Please come in, Sir.' Gabriel bowed, removed his hat, and in the dimness of the lowly, damp dwelling saw a rough looking man, who would be the girl's father, dressed in dirty working clothes. 'Ma. Pa,' said Jane, with overstated care to her diction. 'This is Mr Rose Etty.' Gabriel flourished a bow from the shoulders, but was not asked to sit down, as there were clearly no facilities for entertaining. 'Mr Rose Etty is the painter from London I told you about,' she added.

'Yes. Yes I'd 'eard that much already,' snapped Robert Burden, eyeing Gabriel with suspicion. 'My girl says you want to draw 'er likeness. Is that right?'

Gabriel nodded with another bowing movement. 'I am overwhelmed with Jane's beauty, sir. I am currently engaged in painting frescos from Malory's tales of the Morte D'Arthur on the walls of The Oxford Union Society's new debating chamber in St. Michael's Street. Jane is the perfect model for the Lady Guenevere, so lovely is she.'

'Our Jane lovely? Can't see it meself. Always thought she was a great clumsy clod-'opping girl. And all that hair she got. Cut the lot off and stuff a cushion I'd say.'

'She is unique, Mr Burden. What I would term to be "a stunner". I would be honoured for your permission.'

'And she'll be fully decent and covered up at all times?'

'You have my word. My intentions are strictly honourable.'

'That's as maybe, but she be only seventeen. 'Er sister will 'ave to chaperone 'er.'

'I would be delighted for Bessie to attend with her, Mr Burden.'

'Then I gives my permission, but any nonsense mind, and I'll put an end to it all.' He looked at his hands. ''Ave to go. Got an 'orse wi' strangles.'

The next day Jane and Bessie attended Gabriel's lodgings in George Street, where he received them with exaggerated welcome and hand kissing, but he then set to work with much enthusiasm. Jane was seated on a comfortable chair, her face examined with his index finger, and her chin lifted with the stick handle of a paintbrush. 'I want to get to know your face, your expressions, and your moods,' he said. He re-arranged the position of her head several times, looking intently into her eyes, and telling her, again, that she was the epitome of classic beauty. 'We'll have that hair out of pins and falling to your shoulder. I want a seven-eighths profile, and a plain expression.' As she sat, as still as she could, he scribbled energetically, whistling, muttering and singing.

After half an hour he dropped his charcoal and sat back. 'Hmm. I've not quite caught your aura. Still. Early days.' He unpinned the drawing and showed it to her. 'What do you think?'

Jane contemplated the drawing. 'Is that me? Do I look like that? Is my neck that long? Is my nose so big? Are my eyebrows so thick?'

Gabriel raised her up and led her to a full-length mirror. 'Contemplate yourself, dear Jane. Every inch of you is perfection. The dainty dolls of common taste will fade and grow blowsy, but your beauty will forever delight the eye.'

On leaving the studio the girls walked home arm in arm, and their speech fell back into the stretched vowels of native Oxonians. 'I do believe that Mr Rose Etty is taken in love with you,' Bessie gasped. 'Oh, my dear, can you imagine a life with them sort. Fine food and wines, and gay company, and pretty dresses. What a chance for you to be a lady.'

'He says I am to call him Gabriel,' Jane replied, 'and I do believe I am taken myself with the gentleman. Never has a man looked into my eyes and told me I was lovely.'

'Tell you what. Next time you goes round there I will stay away with a bad cold and he can pay you court.'

Thereafter Jane visited Gabriel alone, and he began a study in oils for her role as the Lady Guenevere, dressed in a flowing white gown, and holding an apple in her hands. After several weeks, during which they had assumed a chaste but close liaison, she arrived to find the work completed. He flourished his hands as he displayed it to her, and declared, 'Your loveliness will indeed be shown for perpetuity, and I have written a few lines in worship.'

'Under the arch of Life, where love and death,
Terror and mystery, guard her shrine, I saw
beauty enthroned; and although her gaze struck awe,
I drew it in as simply as my breath.'

He then took her hand. 'Oh, Janey, Janey. Please forgive my ardour, but I do believe I am suffering from love. I will begin the fresco at The Union next week.' He removed the picture from its stand, turned it over and wrote on the canvas. *To JB, a gift of love from DGR. Beauty enthroned. Oxford Oct 1857.* Jane's journey home was one of dreaming, smiling ruefully, with each slow foot fall accompanied by Gabriel's magical words, "I do believe I am suffering from love".

When Jane arrived at The Union for the first sitting Gabriel hadn't arrived, and she was met by a large, lumbering, untidy man. 'Morris,' he said. 'William Morris.' Jane nodded a greeting to the man. 'Thing is,' he said, 'Gabriel has been called away. His fiancée is reported to be gravely ill.'

Jane, in the throes of shock, swayed. Feeling that she might faint, she threw out an arm and was caught clumsily by Morris. With the confusion of the action a strand of her copious hair had become caught in his fingers, and as he steadied her he carefully tucked it behind her ear, looking at her with an expression of stupefaction. 'Come, Miss Burden,' he said, with gentlemanly solicitude. 'You don't seem well. Take my arm, and I will escort you home.'

Having delivered Jane safely back to Holywell, Morris walked slowly back to the lodgings he shared with Rossetti, in a rare state of calm and wonder, thinking only of Miss Burden's perfection. However, when he arrived his mood was immediately thwarted when he saw Mr Charles Balding, the master Butcher from the covered market, hovering on the doorstep. 'An indelicate matter of settling your very large bill, Mr Morris. I can wait no longer. T'otherwise it's a summons.'

Morris held up his hands, and with his normal characteristic sharp fury returning, shouted out loudly. 'Sir, I have not a penny, and the bounder Rossetti has disappeared. 'Tis him, the glutton, who has feasted so well, not myself. If I pay you in kind will you please get off my back?' He ran into the lodgings and returned with Rossetti's painting of Jane. 'Here. Take this. Mr Rossetti's work fetches a worthy penny. Now be off with you.' The butcher, having had the painting thrust at him, was met with a slammed door in his face.

1957

Polly arrived at Sid's shop as arranged. 'It's all out 'ere,' Sid said, leading him through to a large corrugated iron lean-to at the rear. 'It's a right old pickle. I've put what I reckon to be the best bits at the front, and there's some packing cases over there full of old daubs and picture frames.'

'Right,' replied Polly. 'Get the kettle on, old chap while I have a good shufty.'

Polly saw "it" 'before Sid's back had disappeared. A damaged Victorian frame with cracked glass held a sight that caused a weakness to his knees and a racing of his pulses. Despite its layers of grime he knew it was she! The Stunner! In youth and unique beauty, the delectable, the incomparable, the one and only. Oh, Janey, Janey.

He dragged it over to full light and produced his magnifying glass, and all was as he thought. The brushwork could be by none other than Dante Gabriel Rossetti, and he knew by instinct that it was "right". Signature? Signature? With trembling hands he turned the frame over, and took a knife to the wooden slats so that he could examine the canvas, but before he had a chance to remove it he read the words that nearly caused him to pass out.

To JB, a gift of love from DGR. Beauty enthroned. Oxford Oct 1857.

Polly's heart thumped, and beads of sweat broke out on his brow and lip.

On hearing the whistle of Sid's return with the tea he grabbed an old curtain, flung it round the painting, and placed it behind an old utility sideboard.

'Where did you say all this stuff came from, Sid?'

'Two death clearances, one in Farndon Road, one in Cardigan Street.'

Polly slurped his tea. 'I'm sorry, Sid. There's really nothing here that's jumping out to bite me, apart from this sweet little piece of Crown Derby.'

Sid shrugged. 'Trouble is no-one wants solid quality any more, do they? All the youngsters are moving out to Kidlington, and buying up gaudy stuff with funny shapes and silly little legs. Cheap rubbish. No class. No quality. I reckon our days are numbered. What do I owe you, Poll?'

'Not a penny, but I'll take this little plate off your hands.' Polly put the plate in his pocket and shook hands with Sid. 'Sorry I can't wave a magic wand, old pal. See you tonight for a pint.' As Polly pedalled off his brain was turning like an acrobat. What to do? I've got to get it out of there, and there's no way I'm going halves with dear old Sid on my find of a lifetime.

Minutes later he entered the Old Tom, and collared Bertie Simcock, the landlord. 'A favour, Bert.' He tapped his nose and lowered his eyes. 'It involves some theatricals.' Bertie narrowed his eyes, wondering what sort of wicked wheeze Polly had up his sleeve. 'Have you heard old Sid's had his lease revoked?'

'Yea. I 'eard that the silly arses at the council are going to blitz the area. Grim, innit? Lovely little community. Gawd knows what'll 'appen to my trade. So what's all this favour business about?'

'Right. No questions asked, and Sid mustn't get a whisper I've got anything to do with this. I want you to go round to his shop this afternoon and offer him fifty readies for his entire stock. I'll nip round to the bank in a tick. You swan into the shop casually, say you've just heard from me he's in a jam, and you want to help him out. He'll bite your hand off. Then I'll chip in as a favour by hiring a removal van, and will also offer my services to help load it all up. The whole lot will be shipped out to my lock-up barn in Binsey, and I'll arrange its disposal. You'll get a pay-off of twenty quid, and a free pick of anything that takes your eye from the booty.'

'And I presume that this is after you will have taken your pick of anything well worth having first?'

'You may be right, Bert. Now get me a double scotch.'

The newly found "Janey" painting was duly authenticated as genuine by Sotheby's, and acquired at auction for The Victoria and Albert Museum for a price that exceeded even Polly's estimate. With his new found fortune he bought up a string of leasehold houses in north Oxford, doubling their value five years later by obtaining the freeholds. He then opened his own art gallery in Mayfair, and with an esteemed reputation as a fine art expert, was offered a consultancy at Sotheby's. In the fullness of time he became one of the first regular contributors on the television's favourite antiques programme, where his quick wit and merry personality ensured that he became a much-loved national treasure.

Sid Sparrow, now housed in a council flat on the newly built Blackbird Leys Estate, was blissfully ignorant of his part in Polly's new found wealth and fame, proud in the knowledge that he had personally known the great man in his obscure days. 'Good old, Pol,' he'd say in the pub to anyone who cared to listen to a scruffy old chain smoker. 'Did you see him on the telly last night? My mate, 'e is, from the good old days. Lovely bloke. 'Eart of gold. Do anyone a favour.'

A PERFECTLY MARVELLOUS VIEW

ROSIE ORR

Flavia blotted her lipstick carefully, applied the merest touch of Joy to her wrists and leaned forward to admire her reflection. The recent Botox injections had worked wonders - really, she hardly looked a day over forty - and the new platinum'n'honey highlights - so clever of darling Trevor to have known exactly what would suit her! - set off her positively girlish complexion - the fruit acid peel, though quite hideously painful, had been worth every penny - to perfection.

She glanced at her watch. She wasn't due at the dentist for her check-up - time, perhaps, to discuss a new set of veneers? - for almost an hour; she'd have plenty of time to pop her favourite white Prada trouser suit into the dry-cleaners on the way.

She was about to leave the bedroom - how *did* one keep one's balance in four-inch Louboutins? - when she caught sight of Roger's linen jacket flung on the Louis Quinze love seat by the window. Heavens, it was creased - and more than a little grubby. She frowned. He'd left a smear of toothpaste in the wash-basin this morning, and a wet towel on the floor of the shower - and she'd practically gagged on the smell of that dreadful new aftershave he'd suddenly taken to wearing - so vulgar! What on earth was wrong with the Aqua di Parma she'd given him last birthday?

She'd have to have a word with him when he came home from the office.

Sighing, she picked up the jacket; she'd take it to the cleaners with her trouser suit. She'd folded it up and was about to slip it over her arm when she remembered she hadn't checked the pockets. Hurriedly - it wouldn't do to be late for Mr Patterson - she patted and probed; smiled fondly as her questing fingers encountered various interestingly-shaped objects lying in the satin-lined darkness: this one soft and slippery to the touch (clearly a silk handkerchief); another smooth and cylindrical (obviously a fresh breath spray); a third, a narrow slip of crackling paper (no doubt a receipt for yesterday's business lunch with Ivor, his CEO).

Still, amusing as it was to play guessing games, she had to get on. Upending Roger's jacket over the love seat, she shook it, hard.

Stood staring, rigid with shock, as the contents of his pockets - *one shocking pink satin G-string with torn nylon lace, one orange-smeared Maybelline lipstick case (ugh! TANGERINE TEMPTATION, for heaven's sake!) - one crumpled receipt for a double hotel room* - tumbled out, followed a moment later by a small phial containing Roger's heart pills that had somehow escaped her earlier investigation.

She missed her dental appointment.

In fact she was still sitting on the love seat staring glassily into space when the phone rang on the little table beside her some hours later. She stretched out her hand automatically to answer it; it was Roger, calling to say he'd be late again - 'awfully sorry, darling, but you know how important these Japanese clients are to us' - and not to wait up.

After she'd hung up, her hand shaking now, she began to piece things together: the extraordinarily high number of late meetings there'd been during the last six months - the late night mobile phone calls made in the garden (another business call, I'm afraid, darling - they're hours ahead/ behind in Paraguay/ New Zealand/ Timbuck Bloody Two) - being introduced to Melanie-Jane, his secretary, at the Christmas drinks party. Melanie-Jane, with her gleaming river of ebony hair, her tiny black leather skirt, her enormous breasts barely contained by her lurex boob tube.

Melanie-Jane, with her perfect teeth. Her flawless skin. *Her cheap, bright-orange lipstick.*

It was dark by the time she'd finalised the details of her plan. Through the bedroom window she could see a crescent moon sharp as a nail-paring, the street lights strung along the edge of Hampstead Heath glittering cold as ice cubes. Smiling, she rose to her feet, and stretched; she knew now exactly what must be done. A surprise weekend away was what was needed; a couple of days in a luxury hotel in a city with splendid restaurants, lots of fascinating places to visit and - she smiled, picked up the G-string and gave it an experimental twirl - lots of interesting things to do.

She hurried downstairs to the drawing room, found the newspaper and riffled through the pages of the magazine impatiently until she found the Weekend Breaks section - and there it was, halfway down the page.

Oxford...Five star hotel...Four-poster beds...Log fires...

The Olde English type was superimposed on a photograph of elaborate spires and domes and towers, serene beneath a Wedgwood-blue sky. She peered more closely. Smiled again. It was perfect.

Quite perfect.

By the time Roger got home his jacket was where he'd left it, the contents of the pockets intact. His wife lay propped prettily on her pillows, wearing an all-but-transparent nightdress and a welcoming smile. After they'd made love (which took some time to reach a satisfactory conclusion, Roger having exerted himself excessively earlier that evening) Flavia licked his ear (wincing at the faint whiff of Calvin Klein or whatever it was that still lingered) and whispered that she understood completely and knew exactly what he needed. She'd booked a weekend at a fabulous hotel in Oxford and he was to forget all about everyone at boring old work and simply relax and let her spoil him the way he deserved.

Speaking for herself - she ran a finger slowly up his thigh - she couldn't wait.

They arrived in Oxford early the following Friday evening, and found the hotel without difficulty. It was everything the brochure Flavia had sent for promised; discreet, elegantly appointed, full of quaint little details. Accompanying the brochure was a glossy pamphlet listing some of the city's most popular tourist attractions. Over dinner that night in the hotel restaurant (the promised log fire blazing, candles flickering in pewter sconces on the oak-beamed plaster walls) she slipped it from her bag and laid it beside her plate as Roger swallowed the last spoonful of Death by Chocolate, the quite sinfully delicious dessert Flavia had ordered to follow his canard à l'orange with pommes de terre duchesse. When he'd expressed delighted surprise - the doctor had put him on a strict regime following his heart bypass operation last year, which until now Flavia had insisted he adhere to - she'd laughed gaily and toyed with the small fennel salad she'd chosen for herself. Why, the weekend was supposed to be a holiday! It would do Roger the world of good to forget the silly old diet for once and just enjoy himself. Anyway, who would ever know? It would be their secret. She smiled.

Secrets were such fun, weren't they?

Hardly able to believe his good fortune, Roger agreed with alacrity and ordered extra cream. As the cheese board arrived - heaven! God, how he'd missed a decent Brie! - she laid a perfectly manicured hand on his sleeve. Leaned closer, scooped a generous dollop of the practically liquid cheese onto a deliciously crisp Bath Oliver and held it to his lips. Watched indulgently as he chewed, making little noises of enjoyment, then pushed the brochure across the snowy linen cloth towards him. 'Now, where would you like to go first, darling?'

After breakfast next morning (black coffee and grapefruit for Flavia; full English for Roger, at Flavia's insistence) they set off. The weather was delightful; the sky the precise shade of blue pictured in the Weekend Breaks advertisement, the city bustling (though there was a disappointing absence of gowned and mortar-boarded students cycling enthusiastically to lectures. Clearly they were all in their studies, studying.). A visit to Christ Church soon made up for this deficiency, however; Flavia consulted the guide book as they strolled about, calling out titbits of special interest to Roger's fast-disappearing back - 'Imagine, darling! *Harry Potter* was filmed in this very dining room!' as they entered the magnificent Hall - and, 'Why, Roger! The college choir recorded the theme tune for *The Vicar of Dibley*!' - as they followed a group of nuns through the doors of the Cathedral. Finally they arrived at the gift shop, where she bought a set of table mats and several Harry Potter mugs.

As they walked back up St Aldates, they passed Alice's Shop, where Flavia purchased several more souvenirs - 'I want to remember this weekend forever, darling!' - and smiled lovingly as she took her pile of purchases from the assistant and handed them to Roger.

Lunch at the Randolph (chicken sandwich for Flavia, traditional steak and kidney pudding with twice-fried chips for Roger - 'of course you can, darling, you're on holiday!') was followed by a visit to the Ashmolean Museum, which Roger, making a visible effort - he'd been strangely quiet all morning, almost as if he wasn't enjoying himself - declared stoutly he was definitely looking forward to. Which was a pity, really, thought Flavia (as she lingered in the museum shop, trying to decide between a pair of chunky gold Roman earrings and a silver pomander and eventually deciding to purchase both) since all the galleries turned out to be closed for extensive rebuilding.

Never mind. There was just time for a visit to the Covered Market. When Roger sighed, she reminded him that this wasn't just any old market, for heaven's sake - this market was over a thousand years old, according to the guide book. Why, it was positively historical!

Unfortunately, the bustling market, with its cheerful cafés and stalls piled high with colourful produce, did little to raise Roger's spirits; even the cake shop window crammed with amusingly decorated cakes - there was even one topped with a marzipan boat race, too delightful! - failed to make him smile. If truth be known, he was feeling slightly nauseous. She left him for a moment while she slipped away to buy a simply gorgeous suede shoulder-bag she'd spotted on the way in; when she returned he was gazing morosely at an enormous wedding cake surmounted by a gaily coloured bride and groom. When she tapped him on the shoulder he jumped.

She smiled. 'Time to return to the hotel, darling, if we want to have an early supper before the theatre.'

'Supper?'

'Well, of course.'

He swallowed. 'Lovely. Theatre too, you say.'

'The Playhouse. Special treat - I booked tickets through the hotel.'

He brightened. 'Wow, great. What's the show?'

'*Death Trap*. It's had terribly good reviews, apparently.'

'Can't wait.' He hesitated. 'Thanks for organising this weekend, Flavia.'

'My pleasure. And you know what?' She took his arm. 'It's not over yet.'

The play was a great success, though Roger had cause during the interval to regret Flavia's choice for him at supper earlier of steak and oyster pie with sauté potatoes (she herself having opted for a lightly-grilled plaice). Afterwards they returned to the hotel, and were enjoying a nightcap in the bar when Flavia, nestling close, whispered that she'd got another treat arranged for the following morning. Roger blinked. 'Another... ?' He covered his mouth with his hand to conceal a belch. 'Honestly, Flavia, I don't deserve... '

'I know.'

He turned his head sharply. She smiled, to show she was joking. Watched while he drained his brandy.

'So where... ?'

'A coffee concert at the Holywell Music Room - two dear little string quartets.'

'But you hate - '

'I know, but I think I might enjoy these... they're starting with that famous one, you know - *The Salmon*, or some such. And after that it's - what's it called? Oh yes. *Death and the Maiden*. After that I thought a lovely lunch somewhere, and in the afternoon we could climb St Mary the Virgin church tower - ' She drew the guide book from her sequinned evening bag. 'Look - it's terribly quaint, even older than Alice's Shop, I should think - and it says here that the spiral staircase has a hundred and twenty seven steps. Such fun!'

'A hundred and... ? Come on, old girl, you surely can't be planning to - '

Old girl. How dare he? 'Oh, but we must, darling!' She

smiled. 'I'm sure there'll be a perfectly marvellous view.'

Next morning, after a breakfast of sausages, fried tomatoes and hash browns (Roger) and a single crispbread and a small grapefruit juice (Flavia) they set off for the concert. Fortunately - the waistband of Roger's trousers was now so tight he feared he was in danger of bursting - it was only a short walk to the Holywell Music Room.

Flavia declared the concert great fun, though it was a pity the girl playing the violin had such ghastly hair and if she'd known the seats were going to be so frightfully uncomfortable she'd have taken a cushion.

Afterwards they crossed the road to the Turf Tavern for lunch - such sweet little wooden beams! Though they really should replace the flagstones - an absolute nightmare for anyone in high heels! - where Flavia ordered a green salad sans dressing accompanied by a small glass of pinot noir and insisted that Roger plump for roast beef with all the trimmings plus extra roast potatoes - but they're your favourite, darling! - and sample several of the pub's special ales while he ate. A vast helping of spotted dick and custard followed.

He was paying the bill, having a bit of harmless fun with the pretty young waitress because the stupid card machine wouldn't work, when he looked up and saw Flavia watching, and just for a moment - must have been a trick of the light - he thought she looked positively murderous.

Then she was on her feet. 'Come on, Roger.' She smiled. 'Time for the Tower.'

The old church was gloomy, and musty, and smelled of damp. Several small votive candles flickered in the shadows in front of the rather disappointing altar, and a crowd of Japanese tourists milled about in the gloom. Roger, feeling unpleasantly bloated - perhaps a third Yorkshire pudding hadn't been altogether wise - trailed after his wife towards the gift shop and stood morosely inspecting a rack of postcards while she purchased several glossy books of photographs of Oxford - 'the perfect memento of a perfect weekend, darling!' - and dumped the heavy carrier bag in his arms.

Then she was shepherding him towards the narrow entrance to the tower. The worn steps looked impossibly steep, spiralling upwards into an impenetrable darkness.

'Come along, darling!' Christ, she'd already begun to climb.

A hundred and twenty seven steps.

'Roger?' Flavia's voice floated back to him, echoing, querulous.

With a sigh, he began to climb. Five steps... ten...

Bile filled his mouth, reminding him unpleasantly of the onion gravy that had accompanied the beef; heartburn spread tentacles of fire through his chest. If only he hadn't had those extra potatoes! Said no to the bloody spotted dick Flavia had practically forced on him! Above him her footsteps receded - quick, light. Clinging to the stout blue rope fixed to the wall, he forced himself to go on - he'd never hear the last of it if he gave up now.

Fifteen... twenty...

Sweat beaded his forehead, the tentacles of fire became a band of red-hot agony gripping his chest. Christ, this wasn't indigestion, this was - panicking, he fumbled in his pocket for the phial of pills he always carried. It wasn't there. He had to get out... find help... as he fell to his knees, groaning, he heard the excited chattering of the Japanese tourists as they began to climb behind him, cutting off his retreat.

His left arm was numb; he could no longer grip the rope, or clutch the blasted books. As he began to tumble helplessly down the rough stone steps, a kaleidoscope of vivid images of the enormous meals Flavia had practically forced him to eat began to flicker in front of his eyes - meat smothered in sauces rich with cream - potatoes crisp with lard - suet pastry gleaming with fat - his eyes flew open. Why, it was almost as if -

And then there was only darkness.

Flavia emerged on the balcony at the top of the tower and leant over the balustrade.

She smiled.

The view was perfectly marvellous.

ABOUT THE AUTHORS

Alison Hoblyn is a writer and artist. She has written magazine articles on gardens and their owners, and one novel, *The Scent of Water* (2005), which has a backdrop of Italian gardens. Her latest book, *Green Flowers* (Timber Press, 2009), is a handbook of garden plants. Alison also produces plant-inspired artwork and undertakes commissions. She has lived in and enjoyed Oxfordshire and the city for more than 30 years.

Sheila Costello has had two children's novels published by Oxford University Press: *The Cats'- Eye Lighters* (1991) and *The Box That Joanne Found* (1995), both under the name Anne Lake. Apart from writing, her interests include dancing and music.

Margaret Pelling took half a lifetime to remember that her first love was making up stories. Along the way there was research astrophysics, then the Civil Service, and then one day 'Yes, Minister,' became 'Goodbye, Minister.' Her first published novel is *Work For Four Hands* (Starborn Books), and another publisher has shown interest in the next book, *Capella in Auriga*. What with a couple of other ideas for novels simmering, she's busy at the moment. Her short story *The Rothko Room* was printed in *Mslexia* magazine.

Chris Blount is finally finding time to write more as his career as a private client stockbroker runs down towards retirement.

Jane Stemp published two novels for teenagers, *Waterbound* and *Secret Songs*, with Hodder, in such spare time as she had while working as a librarian for the University of Oxford. She is now a rare books librarian for the Royal Naval Medical Service and, despite an 80-mile weekly commute, has survived being copy-editor of *The Bodleian Murders and other Oxford Stories*. She can be contacted via her agent at David Higham Associates www.davidhigham.co.uk.

Ray Peirson is a prolific and wide-ranging author who has written several full-length novels in various genres – crime, political thrillers, science fiction and also novels for older children - and after an extremely varied career is now writing full-time for publication. His novels are available from Amazon and elsewhere, and he can be contacted at raymondpeirson@btinternet.com.

Linora Lawrence has worked at the Bodleian Library and Oxford University Press, and is now based at Trinity College. She writes for the *Oxford Times* and its magazine *Limited Edition*, besides working on her own stories and a novel. She thinks Oxford still has a wealth of secrets and tales yet to be revealed, and feels it is her task to tell at least some of them. She may be contacted at linoral@gmail.com.

Angela Cecil-Reid spends her days teaching dyslexic children, shepherding rare-breed Cotswold sheep on her farm just outside Oxford, and writing. Her short story *Arthur's Boy* was commended in the Sid Chaplin Short Story Competition, while the opening chapters of her current novel for children, *The Dream Cat*, reached the regional shortlist in Waterstone's Wow Factor Competition.

Jane Gordon-Cumming has had numerous short stories published, and is a contributor to the Romantic Novelists' Association anthology *Loves Me, Loves Me Not*. Her romantic comedy, *A Proper Family Christmas*, was reissued under the OxPens imprint in 2008. Inspired by the success of the OxPens anthologies, she has now written her own collection of ghost stories set on the Oxford Canal, '*The Haunted Bridge' and Other Strange Tales*.

Heather Rosser worked as a teacher in Nigeria and Ghana and as a curriculum writer and journalist in Botswana. On returning to England she set up a language school on the family smallholding in Lincolnshire, and since moving to Oxford has written social studies books for African primary schools. Her first novel was shortlisted for the Constable Trophy but remains unpublished. She has another novel in the pipeline, and can be contacted at www.heatherrosser.com.

Radmila May has lived intermittently in Oxford since 1987. She has had articles published in the literary and political journal

Contemporary Review on subjects including Barbara Pym, the Yugoslav War Crimes Tribunal, and a survey of crime fiction set in Oxford (*Murder Most Oxford*). Her story originated at an Arvon Crime Writing course.

Sylvia Vetta likes to think that she has embarked on her third career after teaching and the antiques trade. In 1998, while a director of Oxford's first antiques centre, in the 'Jam Factory', she began writing the antiques pages of *Limited Edition*, the magazine of the *Oxford Times*. She now writes monthly features in three magazines, having expanded her subject matter to include art, history, fashion, and science-related events.

Gina Claye is a writer and storyteller. Her children's poems have been published in anthologies by Scholastic and Oxford University Press. Her book *Don't Let Them Tell You How To Grieve* (OxPens) is used by Cruse Bereavement Care to help those who are grieving. She gives talks on bereavement to the Hospice Movement, CRUSE and other similar organizations and can be contacted at gina.claye@hotmail.com.

Mary Cavanagh was brought up in North Oxford. She is the author of two novels, *The Crowded Bed* (Transita January 2007) and *A Man Like Any Other* (Matador 2008). In 2009 Troubador published her self-help text book, *A Seriously Useful Author's Guide to Marketing and Publicising Books*. She is a past winner of two short story competitions run by the *Oxford Times* and BBC Oxford/OUDCE.

Rosie Orr lives in Oxford. Since winning the South Bank Show Poetry Competition she has had work published in several magazines and anthologies, including a PEN anthology and *The Virago Book of Love Poetry*. She is currently working on a novel.

We are particularly grateful to Jane Stemp for her skilled and tactful editing. Special thanks as ever to Chas Jones for all his help and advice.

PREVIOUS BOOKS BY OXPENS

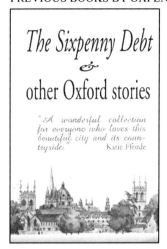

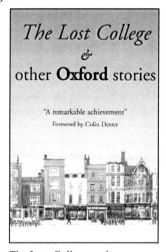

The Sixpenny Debt and
other Oxford Stories

9781904623465

The Lost College and
other Oxford Stories

9781904623120

THESE BOOKS ARE AVAILABLE AS LARGE PRINT VOLUMES

The Sixpenny Debt and other Oxford Stories
9781904623472

The Lost College and other Oxford Stories
9781904623137

The Bodleian Murders and other Oxford Stories
9781904623250

Lightning Source UK Ltd.
Milton Keynes UK
16 November 2010

162944UK00001B/8/P